Casey fell
elevator doors opened.

"Oh, God, thank you. I was so scared!"

Graham held her tight. He rested his cheek against the silk of her hair. He breathed in, deeply, of her scent: soft, feminine, clean. No artificial perfume. He smelled a trace of shampoo that hinted of coconut, but mostly he inhaled the aroma of Casey herself—female pheromones and fragrant skin and just...Casey.

For a long moment, he couldn't speak.

The hit-and-run. The revolving door. The subway threat. Now someone had rigged the elevator doors to jam. If he'd ever had doubts about her first "accident," they were history.

Someone wanted Casey dead.

Now it was his job to find out *why*.

Dear Harlequin Intrigue Reader,

It's the most wonderful time of the year! And we have six breathtaking books this month that will make the season even brighter....

THE LANDRY BROTHERS are back! We can't think of a better way to kick off our December lineup than with this long-anticipated new installment in Kelsey Roberts's popular series about seven rascally brothers, born and bred in Montana. In *Bedside Manner,* chaos rips through the town of Jasper when Dr. Chance Landry finds himself framed for murder...and targeted for love! Check back this April for the next title, *Chasing Secrets*. Also this month, watch for *Protector S.O.S.* by Susan Kearney. This HEROES INC. story spotlights an elite operative and his ex-lover who maneuver stormy waters—and a smoldering attraction—as they race to neutralize a dangerous hostage situation.

The adrenaline keeps on pumping with *Agent-in-Charge* by Leigh Riker, a fast-paced mystery. You'll be bewitched by this month's ECLIPSE selection—*Eden's Shadow* by veteran author Jenna Ryan. This tantalizing gothic unravels a shadowy mystery and casts a magical spell over an enamored duo. And the excitement doesn't stop there! Jessica Andersen returns to the lineup with her riveting new medical thriller, *Body Search,* about two hot-blooded doctors who are stranded together in a windswept coastal town and work around the clock to combat a deadly outbreak.

Finally this month, watch for *Secret Defender* by Debbi Rawlins—a provocative woman-in-jeopardy tale featuring an iron-willed hero who will stop at nothing to protect a headstrong heiress...even kidnap her for her own good.

Best wishes for a joyous holiday season from all of us at Harlequin Intrigue.

Sincerely,

Denise O'Sullivan
Senior Editor, Harlequin Intrigue

AGENT-IN-CHARGE
LEIGH RIKER

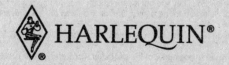

HARLEQUIN®

TORONTO • NEW YORK • LONDON
AMSTERDAM • PARIS • SYDNEY • HAMBURG
STOCKHOLM • ATHENS • TOKYO • MILAN • MADRID
PRAGUE • WARSAW • BUDAPEST • AUCKLAND

ISBN 0-373-22815-5

AGENT-IN-CHARGE

Copyright © 2004 by Leigh Riker

ABOUT THE AUTHOR

Like many readers and writers, Leigh Riker grew up with her nose in a book—still the best activity, in her opinion, on a hot summer afternoon or a cold winter night. To this day, she can't imagine a better combination than suspense and romance.

The award-winning author of ten previous novels, she confesses she doesn't like the sight of blood yet is a real fan of TV's many forensics shows—a vicarious "walk on the wild side," not to mention great research for her own novels. And when romance heats up the mix? It doesn't get any better than that.

Born in Ohio, this former creative writing instructor has lived in various parts of the U.S. She is now, with her husband, at home on a mountain in Tennessee with an inspiring view from her office of three states. She loves to hear from readers! Write to Leigh at P.O. Box 250, Soddy Daisy, TN 37384 or visit her Web site: www.leighriker.com.

Books by Leigh Riker

HARLEQUIN INTRIGUE
772—DOUBLE TAKE
815—AGENT-IN-CHARGE

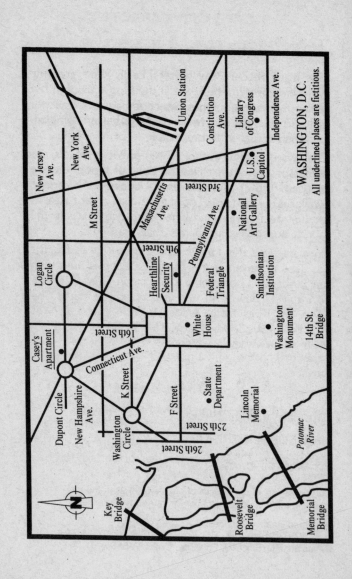

WASHINGTON, D.C.
All underlined places are fictitious.

CAST OF CHARACTERS

Casey Warren—The former art gallery owner's hit-and-run wasn't an accident. Someone wants her dead. Can her ex-husband keep her alive—but will he also steal her heart again?

Graham Warren—Does this mild-mannered civil servant have another, more dangerous, side? Graham isn't talking about his own agenda—or his tangled feelings for the woman he's sworn to protect.

Jackie Miles—Is Graham's sometimes incompetent co-worker part of the solution—or the problem itself?

Sweet William—An aging golden retriever, he is Casey's loyal guide dog. Who just may need her more than she needs him.

Anton Valera—Casey's elderly, and sometimes forgetful, neighbor could be the link to a vicious killer.

Ernest DeLucci—Graham's boss at Hearthline Security, the new government agency. Is he selling secrets to the enemy?

Eddie Lawton—A scrawny techno-wizard with a stubborn cowlick and a nose for other people's business.

Rafe Valera—Anton's son. Friend or foe?

Marilee Baxter—The girlfriend of the hit-and-run driver is filled with remorse. If she's not careful, she could also be dead.

David Wells—This ex-counterterrorism task force member lives beyond his means.

Holt Kincade—The D.C. cop may be moonlighting elsewhere—as a traitor.

Tom Dallas—Graham's former partner. What's a nice guy like him doing in a job like this?

With love
for Don,
Hal,
Kimberly and Tim,
Scott and Linda…
My family, old and new,
who make the world so bright.

Prologue

Casey Warren didn't hear the car at first.

From somewhere above her in the otherwise silent parking garage, its whisper-soft engine made barely a sound. She paid little attention.

At well after five o'clock on a typically hot and muggy summer day in D.C., it was just a car winding its way down the ramp toward the Washington street, its driver eager, as she was, to get home.

Her arms aching from the burden she carried, Casey hurried toward her compact sedan. The sound of her heels echoing on the concrete floor in the almost-deserted garage caused her heart to pound for no reason. Clearly, she'd watched too many movies. *Psycho* had given her an innate fear of the shower curtain being ripped back, a knife flashing in an assailant's hand, and now, the vague sense of uneasiness when walking through a barren garage to her car. Like the film, her fear was unfounded. Silly, to imagine herself as someone being hunted, the innocent prey of a crazed killer.

A half-remembered face flashed through her mind. In the elevator earlier, she'd seen a man who had looked familiar, yet she couldn't place him. Casey had felt uneasy ever since.

Nothing new. Her usual distrust of other people could be bad news or good, depending on the circumstance. From the age of five she'd learned to be self-sufficient to the core. That was the good.

The bad? With her divorce just final, at thirty she was on her own again. Alone.

In the silent garage, that very isolation seemed even worse to her than her recent break from Graham. She didn't need to be surrounded by people, Casey told herself. People she could never quite trust.

For instance, Graham. And—the thought surprised her—the stranger in the elevator who, having caught a passing glimpse of Casey had found her familiar, too. Forget it. Forget them both.

Casey frowned and shifted the box in her arms. Bringing the small carton of Graham's belongings to his office had been something she'd been dreading. He always worked late, and she'd braced herself for a face-to-face encounter. But luck was on her side. She hadn't gained admittance at Hearthline Security once she got there, and she'd seized that excuse to run from the newest government agency.

She didn't really want to see him.

Couldn't risk her heart this soon.

So why had she come in the first place?

Obviously, it was like worrying a sore tooth. Instead, she should have mailed his stuff. Certainly Graham, ever the unflappable civil servant workhorse, would have done that in her place. Just as he'd coolly written The End to their marriage. *What had happened to them?*

Yet despite her own misgivings, she had come, and the nonevent seemed so...final. Too bad she still had the box and all her memories of Graham, with his thick, dark hair, his devil's dark eyes and that quick slash of a grin that always surprised her. Like the way his slightest touch could heat her blood. As if it ever would again.

On level three of the garage Casey turned the corner and spied her car at the end of the row, in the farthest spot from the elevator.

All she heard now was the approaching growl of a big, well-tuned engine.

In that instant the air seemed to fill with sound. The throaty purr of an expensive motor and the shush of tires on pavement reverberated through the quiet parking garage when a long sedan squealed down the ramp, around the curve from the upper level, and screamed onto the third floor.

Inches from Casey's heels.

Too close. *Too close.*

In her peripheral vision, she barely saw it coming. Frozen in shock, Casey felt the big automobile graze her body. Disbelieving at first, she tried to twist aside, but there was no room, nowhere to go except the wall.

The car bumped hard against her side. She bounced off the rear door, spun into the right front fender, then the force of impact lifted her off her feet and she slammed against the hood. For a second her head hit metal. Hard.

Then Casey was thrown back onto the concrete floor.

The car sped away, tires shrieking.

Casey saw a quick blaze of stars.

I'm dead, was her last thought. *I'm dead.*

Then everything went dark.

Chapter One

Total darkness obliterated Graham Warren's senses. Disoriented, he felt his heartbeat kick into overdrive. The acrid scent of burning ash invaded his nostrils, and in the smoky haze he struggled not to cough, even to breathe hard. Any sound might be his last.

Just like Casey—almost—a few weeks ago.

Pushing his way forward into the bombed-out building, he kept his grip tight around his Uzi. His 9-millimeter Glock, tucked into the back of his waistband, would be his backup. Lose that, and he lost himself. His life.

In the blackness he crept forward, keeping his partner behind him. An advance team had already scouted the old apartment building on the fringes of D.C.

Any nagging fears he felt for Casey would have to wait. *He had a job to do.*

Focus.

Complete the mission.

Deliver the remnants of the terrorist cell to the proper federal authorities—

"Psst."

His new partner's voice at his rear stopped Graham.

"What?" He whipped his head around to mouth the word. They weren't supposed to communicate, except in hand gestures. Jackie Miles knew that.

"To the right."

Wishing again that his former partner hadn't been sent to Afghanistan on another assignment, Graham looked in the direction Jackie had indicated and saw a room that had been blasted by the fire into near oblivion. Still, the walls remained.

So did the enemy.

A sudden burst of ammunition nearly shattered Graham's eardrums. They were receiving fire! A shot whistled past his temple, and in a fury Graham pulled his trigger.

Seconds later, the hail of bullets had ended. Their Uzis still ready, his heart still pounding, Graham and his partner edged toward the room where the terrorists had hidden.

Graham steadied his aim.

"Freeze. Put your guns down. Hands in the air. Don't get heroic."

The blasts had already rattled through every pore in his skin, every cell in his body, every nerve ending, every muscle and bone. Most of all, Graham hated the noise, the sharp spurts of automatic fire, the tracers arcing through the night.

Except it wasn't night.

Except for the smoke, it wasn't real.

Tell his heart that, he thought. Tell his lungs.

It would be hours before he unwound.

Graham barged through the barren room. Kicking weapons out of the way, he secured the area. It stunk of creosote and kerosene. Hours before, after some punk had lobbed a Molotov cocktail, the D.C. fire department had issued permission to use the building. The team never knew when an opportunity for such an urban exercise might occur.

Graham barked commands to the mock terrorists. *Up against the wall. Feet spread.* Between them, he and Jackie Miles cuffed the "traitors" with plastic restraints. Other team members moved in to help.

And Graham inhaled his first deep breath in thirty minutes. He was sweating.

His partner laid a hand on his back. "You all right?"

Graham flinched. "Fine. You?"

"Still here. Still breathing."

With that, he dragged her aside. *"What the hell did you think you were doing?"*

Looking away, Jackie holstered her sidearm. "We would have been here all day if I hadn't seen where they were hiding. It's only training."

"Yeah? Tell my churning gut. It could have been the real thing. If it were, we'd both be dead."

Under guard, the "captives" filed past.

Holding his temper in check, Graham finished his duties in record time. Just as he'd raced from Hearthline, leaving the agency's intense security behind as soon as the alert came in. Not secure enough, he thought, but he'd deal with that later. And with Jackie. What was her problem?

His new partner had a thing or two to learn. Still, they had stayed in one piece—and captured the "bad guys." When the time came for a real takedown, they'd be ready.

Graham shook his head. Casey considered him to be just a boring civil servant. If she only knew. Which was exactly the point. She couldn't.

Now that he could breathe again, it wasn't just Jackie who worried him. Or the exercise. For the two weeks since Casey's horrible accident, he'd had a nagging feeling of dread. He had to get out of here. Graham couldn't get it out of his head that she might still be in danger.

He needed to see for himself that she wasn't.

"TELL ME WHAT YOU SEE."

The yellow-gray, elusive blur danced just beyond Casey's wide-open eyes. Innocent and harmless, the light fluttered around the doctor's examination room like a ballerina doing a *tours j'eté* under water. Then it spun away as if on satin toe shoes, trailing gossamer ribbons of remembered sun. Like that imaginary dancer's flowing skirt, the glow was fleeting, graceful…gone.

Casey stared hard at the blank space in front of her. "Nothing," she said, her heart beating hard.

She clenched the edge of the table with—probably—white-knuckled hands. She saw nothing. Felt nothing, except the terror that seemed to follow her everywhere. Without her sight, she felt vulnerable…afraid. Even the antiseptic smells of the office made her nervous. Oh, how she had hoped for better news.

At an unexpected brush of air on her skin, Casey jerked back on the exam table. The doctor had passed a slow hand in front of her face, that was all. She had to get hold of herself.

"Shapes?" he said. "Do you see any shapes?"

She shook her head. "No. Just the flickering light sometimes." Rarely.

In the hospital that first day, her whole body had hurt but Casey's vision seemed fine. Then a few days later, it blurred, dimmed. From there, her eyesight had gone downhill. Was this all she could expect, forever?

Fresh anxiety ripped through her.

Her future promised—no, threatened—*total darkness,* her own terrors locked inside her like a scream. She didn't know where the next thought came from. Certainly she didn't want it. *I'll never see Graham's face again.*

She squeezed her eyes tight, turning the darkness into a blood-red sunset behind her lids, and conjured him mentally—dark hair and eyes, that handsome face and beloved smile, broad shoulders and tough, lean body so at odds with his sedentary job pushing papers at Hearthline.

Casey bit back tears. "I should get myself a guide dog, what do you think? A nice big German shepherd…." With teeth like razors.

She loved animals. She'd always wanted a dog, but not under these circumstances. How would she take care of it now? Take care of herself? She couldn't do this, wouldn't survive on her own this time.

The doctor patted her shoulder but said nothing more. Which, for Casey, said it all. *Poor thing.* She hated pity.

"Try to be patient," he said. "You never know in cases like these. It can take time."

Casey couldn't cling to false hope. "I doubt time will help. You said I had some kind of delayed hemorrhage."

"Yes, that happens sometimes after a frontal head trauma. Edema within the optic nerves leads to—"

"I know what it leads to." Casey touched a hand to her forehead, where some of the worst bruises had been. They were healed, but her eyes were not. She made herself say the words through tears. "I'm *blind*."

Bilateral blindness. Both eyes.

He didn't try to contradict her. When the doctor slipped out of the room to make her next appointment, he left Casey defenseless in the blackness from which there would be no escape. She was alone inside herself. And still terrified, not only because of her blindness.

In Casey's mind getting run down in that parking garage had been no accident. To her, that meant only one thing. Someone—the same someone who had blinded her—would try again to kill her. And now she couldn't protect herself.

Ironic, really, when she had prided herself on not needing anyone, especially Graham.

But it wasn't Graham she "saw" now. Another face, unsmiling, flashed through her mind. When she'd been in pain, she had suppressed the memory of the man she'd seen in the elevator at Graham's office building. Pale hair, pale features, she remembered. Why think of him again now? Was he harmless, just an acquaintance she couldn't quite place—or part of the threat she continued to feel?

The fear raced through her again like another speeding car bent upon her total destruction. When it happened the next time, she wouldn't be able to see it coming.

IN THE LOBBY of her doctor's building where he'd been waiting, Graham was relieved to see Casey finally emerge from the elevator. She wasn't alone.

Graham nodded at the nurse then focused on Casey.

"Hey, babe." He swallowed. "How'd it go?" He had heard the tap of her white cane before he actually saw her, but he could tell by her face that she'd had bad news. Casey didn't hide her emotions as well as Graham did these days. She hadn't walled them up inside.

Startled by his voice so near, Casey missed a step and Graham cursed himself. He hadn't meant to surprise her. Briefly, her head tilted in his direction. Then she kept walking, the cane that had become an extension of her right hand in the past few weeks rhythmically tapping the Carrara marble floor.

"It's a miracle," she murmured in the too-light tone she sometimes used to downplay a problem, as she walked right past him. "I can see, I can see."

Obviously, she couldn't, and sudden anger swept through him. Graham glanced again around the busy lobby of the professional building, making sure it remained secure. For the past half hour, after his quick stop at home to shower away the smell of smoke and change clothes, he'd made regular checks of the area from his leaning stance against the marble wall. But, like Jackie Miles's earlier blunder, he couldn't quell his own uneasiness about Casey.

Graham peeled himself away from the wall. "I'll take care of her," he said to the nurse after introducing himself. When Casey didn't object, he waited again while she thanked her doctor's nurse, who gave Graham a crisp goodbye. And another thorough once-over as if to reassure herself that she was leaving Casey in good hands.

Graham watched the woman disappear into the elevator.

Casey wouldn't welcome him fussing over her, either. Yet she needed someone right now—in this case, him.

He stepped in front of her, forcing Casey to halt when she would have struck off on her own.

"Tell me what he said."

She gazed sightlessly at the floor between them.

"He said, 'be patient.'"

Her sleek blond bob had slipped like silk around her pale cheeks, creating a heavy curtain that hid her smooth, even features. Her straight little nose. Her beautiful green eyes were hooded by her lids now, and she didn't try to look at him, which made him all the more angry. With her, with himself. They might not be married any longer but...

"Casey. Don't. It's me."

And he watched her crumple. Just like that.

She didn't want to, he guessed, but she flowed like warm honey into his waiting arms.

To his surprise, Graham felt a flash of familiar but unwelcome desire run through his body. With their first touch, he had caught fire—like that run-down apartment building for the team exercise. Graham tried to tamp it down, but Casey, slender yet curvy in all the right places, her skin warm and as soft as down, felt like home in his embrace. Hell. What was he doing, lusting over a broken woman? A woman who didn't belong to him now?

"It's over," she said against the front of his dress shirt. He felt wetness seep through the blue cotton. "I'm trapped inside myself. I've never liked small, enclosed spaces, but now that's all I have. I'll never be able to run an art gallery of my own again. Never see the paintings on the walls. The colors. Never know if something is good, or bad. How could I now?"

Graham shut his eyes, sharing the darkness with her for a moment. "You'll find a way. You know you will."

He had to remind himself that they were quits. *Over*, as she'd said of her gallery.

His remark seemed to stiffen her spine, but he hated seeing her like this, hated knowing what someone else had done to her in that lonely parking garage. To Casey, her career, her life, her future had been snatched away along with her vision.

And her accident still troubled him, too.

That was natural.

She had nearly been killed.

But why in hell had the accident happened in the first place? Mere steps from his own office at Hearthline?

He took another look around the lobby. When he saw nothing suspicious, Graham tipped up her chin so he could look into her eyes, and the pain ripped through him all over again. *Her gorgeous green eyes.* Hell, he could do this much for her if nothing more.

"Let me take you home. My car's outside."

Casey pulled away, then set her shoulders. "I may be blind. I'm not crippled. I am fully capable of leaving this lobby and raising a hand to call a cab." She stepped back a few inches. "You have no responsibility for me, Graham, remember? Our marriage is over."

"We're divorced, not mortal enemies." Which only made Graham angrier at himself. "Frankly, if you ask me, you could use not only a lift—you could use a friend."

"You are not my friend."

Ouch, he thought, but he knew he hadn't acted like a pal, much less a husband. He couldn't fault her for not trusting him, for walking out. He'd driven her to it.

Yet Graham would be the first to admit that things weren't always what they seemed. Including him. Too bad he couldn't tell Casey anything—for now— but lies.

He double-checked the lobby, finding only the normal flow of passersby intent upon their errands. It didn't soothe him. He forced his tone to sound lazy, nonthreatening. He wanted to get her out of here.

"Listen, friend or not, I've got a great car. Leather seats. Air conditioning. I haven't had a speeding ticket in, oh, three or four weeks." Since before Casey was hurt, the last time he'd felt able to unwind. "Take a chance, babe. Sit back and enjoy. I'll have you home in fifteen minutes. Less, if we hit the lights right."

Safe, he thought. If only, as he'd planned, he could have kept her safe....

Casey raised her face to his.

"Thank you very much, but I can find my own way home."

Graham's mouth tightened. *Like hell you will.* When she started to tap-tap her way toward the revolving doors, he stood there for a moment, staring, before he went after her. He couldn't help feeling thwarted—and for some niggling reason he couldn't define, still afraid for her.

He took one step before he felt the very air around him grow thick, heavy, with an ominous portent that seemed to smother him—and at the same time to shout a warning.

"Casey!"

Too late. Helpless, Graham watched it happen. One second she was making her way to the revolving doors, probably guided to their location by the constant swish of movement she heard as people came and went. In the next instant Casey had been shoved into a moving door. From the sidewalk, a man in dark clothes sent the door spinning, circling, round and round and round with Casey trapped inside.

Breaking into a run, Graham hurdled a woman's stroller carrying a small child and twisted to avoid a pair of startled businessmen. His heart threatened to burst in his chest. *Out of my way, damn it.* All he could think was, *Trust the feeling. I was right.* He had known something bad would happen. He had to get to Casey....

CASEY'S CRIES echoed through the vaulted lobby. By now, she didn't know up from down, in from out. Her world of darkness whirled. Played havoc with her sense of balance.

She tried to brace herself but felt like a rag doll being flung by a furious child from one side of the constantly circling space in which she was caught to the other. Over and over. Her head spun. Her own voice shrieked, and sound shattered. First she heard the swish of the revolving door, then a wedge of traffic noise. Blaring horns. Screeching brakes. A few footsteps passing by. Then that pressured silence again, like being shut inside a vacuum.

Casey couldn't tell where she was. In the spinning section of the door her shoulder hit one glass partition then another, hard, her bones and muscles throbbing on impact.

The whole terrifying incident happened in less

than a minute, but all the while she could sense the
man who stood outside, preventing her escape. She
could imagine the Grim Reaper smile on his lips. Her
blood rushed through her veins, the memory of her
"accident" roared through her mind again. *Was it
the man from the elevator?* She tried to fight back,
to push against the glass, but without effort he only
shoved the door. Harder.

GRAHAM'S PULSE hammered. He raced across the
lobby in seconds that seemed like a lifetime. Charg-
ing out onto the sidewalk, he stopped the man's arm
on the upswing before he could push the revolving
door again. Then Graham lowered his shoulder and
charged, trying to butt him. The guy sidestepped him
and Graham missed. Bastard.

He was solid, well-muscled. So was Graham,
but before he could recover his own balance, the
guy was gone. Graham hadn't even seen his face.
Casey, who had been flung out of the revolving
door when Graham's arrival slowed its motion, was
lying on the sidewalk. By that time a crowd had
gathered.

"Somebody help her!" he shouted then took off
to prevent the guy's escape. Graham did his best
imitation of a linebacker, snaking his way through
the puzzled crowd, breathing in sharp hisses like a
set of air brakes. Heads turned, necks craned at him
and the man he was chasing down the busy Wash-

ington street, but Graham's hours in the Hearthline gym were no match for his heart-pounding terror.

He was still ten yards away when the man, a blur of black pants and shirt, knocked a male pedestrian aside. He vaulted into a dark car at the curb, then tore off, literally. On his way out of the space he bashed the left rear fender of the SUV parked in front of him. Metal crunched. A taillight splintered. A passing taxi horn blew, the cab narrowly missing the car that peeled off into traffic. Then there was silence. Eerie silence.

Graham no longer heard the rush of passing vehicles, the growing buzz of conversation. He bent over, hands braced on his thighs, and gulped in the smoggy, humid air until he could breathe. Then he jogged back to Casey, now sitting on the pavement looking dazed.

Several people hovered over her, offering handkerchiefs and sanitary hand cleaner. Graham bent down to her. Casey's palms and knees were scraped raw, oozing blood, and fresh anger spurted through him.

"Damn. Come on, babe, let's get out of here."

With thanks for the small group of passersby who had come to her aid, he gently helped Casey to her feet. Graham should have trusted his instincts. Divorced or not, whether or not she trusted him, he needed to see her safe at home. Then he needed to start asking hard questions. He hadn't wanted to think the hit-and-run was deliberate, but now he would learn the truth—all of it.

Maybe then he could tell her the truth about himself.

"YOU SURE YOU'RE OKAY?" he asked Casey.

They had reached her apartment near Dupont Circle, but Casey was still shaking. Hadn't she known someone would try again to hurt her?

"I'm okay," she tried to assure Graham when he could see that she was not. He could *see*.

Digging in her bag for her key, she held it out to him. She wouldn't be able to fumble it into position herself. Let him do it. Just this once.

Casey even allowed herself a brief, familiar fantasy. Less than a year ago they might have come home like this from a rare evening out, probably at some government function. Still in his tux, his dark hair glossy, his eyes hot, his sensual mouth curved in an always surprising smile, Graham would curl up beside her on the sofa for a nightcap. One thing would lead to another... They'd make lazy love then fall asleep in each other's arms, warm, sated, only to wake the next morning with their clothes strewn all around the room. And they'd make love all over again.

Casey shook herself. That was all in the past. Graham was the last man she could be intimate with now, even if he was the only one who made her feel safe.

These familiar surroundings didn't quell her anxiety. The smells of cooking that drifted from other apartments, the blast of someone's television, the feel of the floor beneath her feet in the hallway could lead to fresh terror in a heartbeat.

As panic engulfed her, she had to suppress the impulse to throw herself into Graham's arms again. That would create a danger of a different kind. She couldn't get near Graham without noticing his scent, his body heat, the deep timbre of his voice that heated her blood.

Maybe she shouldn't have taken Graham up on his offer of a ride home. But her nerves were shot. She kept remembering those frightening seconds in the revolving door, being spun out of control. Every sound, even the scrape of the key in the lock, set her heart racing again. Who might be lurking around the nearest corner? Ready to attack her again? To *kill*.

Graham couldn't slip the key into the lock fast enough for Casey. Then he said, *"Wait. Don't go in."*

And in the entryway, she could feel it, too, that sixth sense that they weren't quite alone. Then suddenly, they weren't.

The door across the hall flew open and footsteps pounded toward her. Casey felt a heavy hand settle on her shoulder. "What's wrong here?"

The dark voice belonged to her neighbor, but not to her elderly and sometimes forgetful neighbor. It was Anton's son, big Rafe Valera. Wide-shouldered, thick-muscled, a bull of a man with dark hair and hard gray eyes. To Casey he'd always been as gentle as a kitten without claws.

Graham disagreed. Without warning he slammed Rafe up against the doorframe. *"Drop it."*

"Damn it," Rafe bellowed, "you almost broke my arm!"

Casey heard a brief scuffle, some kind of karate throw, then a few grunts before something heavy, like metal, thudded to the floor.

Graham's voice was a low-pitched snarl. "This jerk was carrying a gun."

A gun? Rafe owned a gun?

"I heard noise," he said. "I was worried about Casey."

The two men knew each other slightly but Casey felt their usual instant dislike in the air. Once, that would have meant jealousy on Graham's part. She thought of Rafe's dangerous good looks, his usual black clothes.

"You remember Rafe," she said, which didn't lighten Graham's mood.

"Does he always flash a .357 Magnum when he sees you?" Clearly disapproving, Graham disappeared inside to check the apartment. Then he was back, prowling the living room while she and Rafe hovered in the open door, silent with tension.

When Casey heard her answering machine click on not ten feet away, she jumped. "Listen to this," Graham muttered.

She frowned, puzzled. It was only her doctor's receptionist with a reminder message from yesterday about her appointment today. "What is it?"

"Someone was here."

She'd been right and Casey sounded braver than she felt. "The man who pushed me into the revolving door?" She could feel Rafe's sharp eyes on her but didn't stop to explain her latest mishap. "You mean, he heard the message. Then he knew where to find me."

"And followed you there," Graham agreed. "There are no visible signs of forced entry. There isn't a chair out of place, nothing disturbed." This only seemed to make him more suspicious. "Valera, did you see or hear anything?"

"I was about to wake my father from his afternoon rest before Casey got home. I didn't hear or see a thing until you came."

Graham returned his attention to Casey. "When you weren't here at the apartment earlier—thank God, you weren't—your visitor must have split. Apparently he got exactly the information he needed."

The other apartment door opened again. Casey heard Anton's carpet slippers shuffle across the hall. The older man sounded frantic. His European accent had deepened.

"What is happening? I wake up from my nap and Rafe is gone." She envisioned Anton's graying hair, standing on end, his blue eyes fierce. "You are not hurt again, Casey?"

"No." Not too much. "I'm fine." She reached out a reassuring hand, and heard Rafe bend down to retrieve his gun. Graham didn't stop him, but his tone stayed grim.

"I'll talk to you later, Valera. You too, Anton." He waited until they went back across the hall. Then he ushered Casey inside and locked the door.

"If I had any doubts before about your hit-and-run being deliberate, Casey, I don't now. Ever since the revolving-door incident, I've been wondering if the guy saw me with you in that lobby. If he did, then why risk going after you?" Graham paused. "Now I wonder if he *did* see me—and wanted us to know that you aren't safe, even with someone else around. That you're a target even in a crowd."

Casey shivered. "Because I'm…blind."

"I think he wants us to know you're always alone in that way, always vulnerable. And he can get to you. No matter where you are."

Us? "Then earlier he didn't mean to kill me."

"It was a warning," Graham suggested. "But why?"

Without thinking, Casey took a step forward. Graham moved, too. Then she was in his strong, hard arms, held tight to his broad chest. Graham pressed his cheek to her hair.

"What the hell is going on?" he muttered.

Casey didn't know. Yet even here, in her own home, she wasn't safe. Until she learned why, she wouldn't forget those terrifying moments caught in the whirling doors.

Just as she couldn't forget the man in the elevator.

Or being run down like some hunted prey.

Chapter Two

The next morning when Casey's doorbell buzzed, her heart beat so fast it threatened to shatter. She felt her pulse in the still-stinging scrapes on her hands and knees. After yesterday's twin mishaps, she stood frozen with one hand on the doorknob. Outside she could hear someone breathing heavily.

He wants us to know you're alone...vulnerable.

What if her attacker was just inches away, with only the closed door between them and her possible murder?

"Casey, open up. It's okay."

Graham. Still, Casey hesitated. Last night she had stayed in Graham's embrace until she finally stopped trembling, automatically seeking solace in his familiar scent, and the safety she found in his arms. She refused to let him stay the night, then hadn't slept a wink after he left.

Casey fumbled the locks open. "What are you doing here again?" She heard something whap, hard and rhythmically, against the nearby wall. Then something warm and moist nudged her side.

"I brought you a present." Graham stepped into the apartment. His arm brushed hers for a fraction of a second, and a disturbing tingle of awareness ran over her skin. "The wet nose comes with the dog." Casey heard the sharp click of toenails on her entry floor. "Meet Sweet William," Graham said.

"A guard dog?"

For an instant she preferred that to Graham's scent, his touch, his masculine aura. The too-vivid memory of his dark hair and eyes, that hot gaze that would send desire racing through her body. Even without her sight, she had perfect recall of his high-chiseled cheekbones, his broad shoulders, his muscled chest, his washboard belly, strong tanned hands and powerful thighs. She didn't have to see, Casey realized, to get the same effect. The flesh on her bare arm still buzzed from their brief contact.

"A guide dog," Graham corrected.

But she didn't want his help. Somehow she had to pick up the pieces of her own life and go on. Only yesterday she'd learned that her blindness might be permanent. In the doctor's office she'd considered the possibility of getting a dog, maybe even the eventuality, but her comment then had been facetious, a quip to keep her from falling apart. For weeks she'd held the hope of a complete recovery. She wasn't ready to consider the full impact of her situation.

Leaving Graham and the dog to follow, Casey inched, one hand braced on the wall, into the living room. Twelve paces to the sofa, she remembered, not letting her skin graze Graham's again. But she couldn't avoid inhaling the clean-soap smell of him. Which only hardened Casey's resolve.

She would try to retain some of the independence she'd lost with her sight. Take care of herself.

As if to disagree, Sweet William padded right behind her. With that name alone, how could she feel afraid?

Graham steered her to a chair, and Casey struggled not to feel that same jangling awareness when his soap-scented skin met hers. She felt the heat of his hand against her back and the slow burn flared deeper in her abdomen.

"Last night," Graham began, "I made some telephone calls. Finally one of my contacts led me to the Guide Dog Institute. This morning the director told me they have a waiting list a mile long, that there was no hope of getting a dog any time soon. But then he remembered Willy. He's a golden retriever and highly trained," Graham went on. "But he's getting along in years. Because of his age, the institute decided to retire him. He's out of the program now and he's been up for adoption, more as a pet or companion, but so far no one has taken him."

"I can't, either," Casey murmured.

She heard the irritation in his tone. "No? From

what I told him, the director seems to think you and Willy might make a good match. He let me pick him up today for a trial. Listen," Graham said, "just keep him for a few days and see how it goes. I'll buy some dog food, a bed, whatever else he needs. You can get to know each other. And, oh," he added, as if he'd just thought of it, "the institute will throw in some training lessons. Normally their program is pretty rigorous and intense, but he thinks you can learn the basics in a week or two. I took the liberty of signing you up for a first session."

"You did?" Casey sighed in frustration. "Does the word *divorce* hold any meaning for you?"

"Oh, yeah." He didn't sound happy. "Just because we're divorced doesn't mean I have to quit worrying about you."

"I don't need your concern."

"After yesterday? Great." She heard him drop onto another chair, clearly intending to stay. At the same time Willy apparently decided to lie down next to Casey. He circled a few times, raising the air around her with the musky scent of dog, grunted once, then settled down. She heard him breathing.

Graham tried again. "Casey, take the gift. I know damn well you're scared—not just about this vision loss, but about what caused it. The question remains, why did these 'accidents' happen?"

Casey had no idea, but with Graham's mention of the attacks, she felt another emotion. The anger felt welcome, fresh and cleansing. "I may be afraid, but I'll never see the people I love again. I'll never run through a field. I can't even play Frisbee with this dog. And one day ago my home was invaded, Graham. Do you know how that felt?" She wrapped her arms around herself. "Like a violation. Well, I've had enough. I'm going to find out who's responsible."

"Not by yourself, you're not."

"I suppose that's true," she admitted. "Did the police find any prints here last night?"

Graham had called some law enforcement contact of his, which in itself came as a surprise to Casey. He was full of them. The woman who showed up had been efficient, collecting samples, vacuuming the carpet for trace evidence, and slipping her other rare finds into little bags while Casey wondered how Graham knew such people.

"They're still working on the fingerprints. She lifted a partial but it could be another of your prints, mine, Anton's..." He hesitated. "And what about Rafe Valera?"

Casey frowned. "I doubt it. He's only been in my apartment once or twice."

"That's enough." She could sense the same scowl on Graham's face. "He raises the hairs on the back of my neck. With very little provocation he showed up here yesterday waving a gun. A big gun. He looked like he knew how to use it."

"He only wanted to protect me."

"Did he?" Obviously, Graham wasn't that sure. "I know you and the old guy have become close. Anton makes a great father surrogate, but his son is another matter. Casey, be careful. I think he's dangerous. Until I ask around about Rafe Valera, it may be wiser to avoid him."

"You can't think Rafe had anything to do with the break-in here, or my experience in the revolving door?" She wouldn't even think about the hit-and-run.

"How well do you really know either of the Valeras?"

"Not that well but—"

"Then just be careful," he repeated. "Some extra caution wouldn't hurt, Casey. I want you protected. I don't want you living alone. Until we figure this out, Willy can help minimize the danger." Probably to distract her, he returned to their earlier discussion. "He can help you adjust to your condition in lots of ways." Graham paused. "And—quid pro quo—you'll be helping him."

As if to confirm that, Willy wiggled closer, and Casey's hand bumped against warm, silky fur. In spite of her earlier concerns, she stroked him—and felt a strange feeling wash through her. She wasn't alone. Casey almost welcomed the subject of the dog's welfare.

"Me? Help him? How?" she asked. "He's the one who can see where he's going. You just said—"

"He had the same owner for six years until the guy passed away a month ago. William is now eight years old. If he doesn't find a new home soon, he's going to be in serious trouble."

That struck a chord with Casey, as Graham knew it would. After her parents died when Casey was five, she'd been juggled from one relative to another, never quite belonging anywhere. For a while, in Graham's arms, she had hoped...but that hope had died. Casey petted Willy's fur but felt she was stroking Graham's skin instead. She pulled her hand back.

Her heart lurched. *You poor thing.* They were two of a kind. Again, she reached out a comforting hand. A wet nose met her palm and Willy licked her, twice. "Not fair, Graham. You know I'm a sucker for animals."

"He's grinning," Graham said in a coaxing tone that went straight through her like a caress. "He likes you."

"This is fighting dirty. You know that, don't you?"

"He has great eyes," Graham murmured. "Dark, liquid—" Like Graham's, she thought. "Full of trust," he added, which shattered the illusion. Trust didn't come easily to Casey, especially where Graham was concerned. "He's got a hundred-yard stare. Just the thing you need for protection."

Willy seemed to know that, too. With another grunt he lumbered to his feet, then laid his head in her lap.

Graham knew he had her. He'd be wearing his own, surprising grin now, the one that shot her defenses every time. Casey ran both hands over Willy's silken ears, feeling the tufts of hair, then smoothing his bony forehead. She could feel him gazing at her, hoping. Perhaps even, if dogs were so inclined, praying.

Graham closed in for the…kill. "He always wears this goofy grin unless he's really concentrating on the job. Then, kind of like me, I swear he frowns. He has terrific hearing, and even better instincts. By tomorrow, you're gonna thank me, Case."

But, as he well knew, she was hooked. With his head in her lap, Sweet William had won her heart. Just like Graham, the first minute she saw him. Tall, dark and dangerous, she'd thought then, losing herself in his smoldering eyes anyway.

But Graham, she had learned, posed little threat. He was normally as steady as a concrete pillar. He never took unnecessary risks, except with his driving. Hearthline relied on him to handle government paperwork with more dedication than he'd shown for their marriage. Casey supposed the only true danger he posed was to her own still-hurting heart.

Be careful.

Maybe until she found the reason for the attacks on her, Willy could help allay her fears.

"You won't have to wait." Feeling her way, she stroked Willy's broad back then planted a kiss on the top of his head. She could all but hear his tongue lolling in delight. "Like your new home, pal?" Casey lifted her sightless gaze in Graham's direction. "I'm already in love. You rat…thank you."

"How did she take it?"

Slow to answer, Graham watched Jackie Miles lean back in her seat across from him and grin. He didn't smile back. Even after chewing Jackie out about the training exercise yesterday, he still felt edgy. He could see Casey last night, looking pale, could feel her in his arms at the doctor's building beforehand. He could see her melting over Willy earlier that day, yet trying to hide her fears.

"How do you think?" he said.

Her grin widened. "She kept him, though. Right?"

"Right."

Jackie ran her fingers through her short red hair. "So why the frown, tough guy? Casey has a dog to help her. And Willy has a place to live—literally."

Graham lifted his eyebrows. In frustration, he tapped a pen against the edge of the table. They were alone in the booth of a small diner not far from Casey's apartment, and were the only customers in the place, yet he could feel danger in the air.

"Watch it," Graham murmured. "Be careful what you say."

When her brown eyes cooled, he decided that he

missed his original partner, Tom Dallas, who had gone back into the field about the time Graham and Casey split up.

Then there was Casey herself.

Graham kept his tone low.

"Before I hooked her up with the dog, she was depending on the old man across the hall—a nice enough guy but he's seventy-five if he's a day. Not much protection there." Graham sighed, then, in an even softer voice, told Jackie the little he knew about the man's son, Rafe Valera. "I was a hair away from pulling this out—" he patted his coat over his Glock "—when the old guy showed up. If we're right about her first 'accident' and the revolving-door episode, then she's still at risk. I'm not always around to make sure nothing happens to her."

"You're divorced, boy-o."

"So she keeps reminding me."

She laid a hand on his arm.

"You're not responsible for her any longer."

"So she told me."

When he pulled his arm free, Jackie swiveled away to reach for the sugar, as if he'd rejected her, and Graham changed the subject again. It wasn't comfortable for him, either, admitting his marriage had gone belly-up.

No sense jumping down Jackie's throat again about Casey, when what she'd said was true. He needed Jackie to help him crack a difficult case, the reason they were sitting now in a diner several miles from the Hearthline complex to have a private conversation.

Graham's personal life might be a mess, but he couldn't afford to screw up this latest assignment. Casey's well-being was one thing—and important to him. National security was another, and Graham returned to the business he shared with Jackie. Cloak-and-dagger, he thought. They were even "hiding" in a corner so as not to be overheard.

"Find anything new in those telephone logs or cell phone records?" He didn't mention Hearthline by name.

"De nada," Jackie answered, still with her profile to him. "Our guy is a real closemouthed type."

"He's careful, that's for sure. I've been running the e-mail search myself." The pen rapped the table edge again. "Nothing there, either. Hell, the breach has *got* to be someone in the agency."

Jackie faced him again. "True, but weird." Hearthline's motto was "The Bastion of National Security." "Selling secrets to Al-Hassan or any other terrorist network must be highly profitable—and it makes our guy on the inside a traitor."

Graham frowned at his pen. Their mission hadn't proved easy, not that he expected it to be. But locating the source of a major security leak before it triggered another terrorist attack on the U.S. was proving even more elusive than he'd thought.

"He's there all right. I can feel it." He rubbed the

back of his neck. "What we don't know is who he is."

"I have a theory you might like," Jackie murmured and Graham's head shot up. She silently mouthed the name *Eddie Lawton.*

"The IT guy?" He'd fixed Graham's computer once. A small, scrawny kid with big glasses, a stubborn cowlick and a pen protector in his pocket.

"He's a techno geek, I know. That's why he's perfect. PC's are his friends, better than people to him. He looks harmless, even cute—" Jackie shuddered "—but it would be first-grade easy for him to hack into the databases. Believe me."

"Maybe so, but I still think it's someone higher up." Graham had been making a list right before he suggested they go for coffee to discuss matters. Before he'd reamed Jackie about the training exercise. Before she'd brought up Casey. "Much higher," he said.

Jackie saw his point. "You mean, someone privy to real information as it comes in."

Like DeLucci. The thought of their boss soured Graham's stomach.

"Right, and with the alert at highest level—"

"'Rumor has it another disaster on a massive scale is all but imminent.'" She quoted their supervisor's latest memo. "Thanks to whoever-the-hell-it-is we're looking for. High or low." She stirred the sugar into her coffee. "Whoever it is, we'll find a slip or a name somewhere in those records—and then a face to go with it."

Graham set his cup aside. "We'd better get started."

"I have more cell phone calls to wade through before quitting time." She leaned close to whisper, "And that's our exciting life, 007. Sometimes I think the undercover drudgery at M-6 will kill me before a traitor's bullet can."

Graham pushed back in his seat. Their true affiliation was not with Hearthline, but with C.A.T., a top-secret, elite counterterrorist team funded in part, it was said, by the CIA.

"Listen." He checked the narrow room again, finding no other patrons at the moment. "This diner is better than a 'dedicated' huddle room at the agency, but still, no exception. The walls could have ears, so watch it. Let's go."

Graham slipped his pen into his jacket. He wouldn't dwell on the fact that his marriage may have gone bust because of his job. That he'd lost Casey, who found it hard to trust in the first place, precisely because he had been lying to her about who he was and what he did.

Yet one question had been teasing the edges of his mind ever since he'd gotten the call that Casey was hurt.

Graham paid for their coffee, ushered Jackie outside then posed the question. "Here's another thing to chew on. What do you suppose *she* was doing at my office that day?"

And *why* had Casey been run down less than a block away, of all places in the nation's capital?

Walking beside him to his car, Jackie shrugged. "She wanted to see you, obviously."

Graham shook his head. "I had distinctly told her never to go there, but why in hell would someone want to hurt her?"

"Or try to kill her," Jackie murmured.

Exactly. Graham's blood chilled at the thought.

Like hell Casey was no longer his responsibility!

Until her assailant was caught, Graham, just like Sweet William, was there to stay.

He couldn't stop the thought: *And to keep her alive.*

Chapter Three

"Tell me again. Everything that's happened since you went to my office."

Graham paced in front of Casey's living room sofa where she sat with Willy at her feet. Every step Graham took carried his scent to her nostrils, made her pulse rise another notch.

"If we kick this around enough," Graham insisted, "we may find a reason for the attacks on you."

As he spoke, she tried even harder not to recall her last sight of his long, lean body, his dark hair and eyes, his high cheekbones. She didn't need her eyesight to know he wasn't wearing that surprising grin now.

Casey rested a hand on Willy's warm shoulder and went through her story one more time. Her drive to Graham's office—her last drive on her own—the elevator ride upstairs, then leaving for the garage, hearing the speeding car too late. The sketchy details never seemed to satisfy Graham. He insisted they were missing something that could tell them *why* she had become someone's target.

"Again," he said when she finished for the third time. "You were at Hearthline in the first place because…?"

"I know you told me never to go there." Casey sensed he was not only frustrated by the lack of information she could supply but also irritated. So was she. "Too bad. It wasn't enough that you spent the bulk of your time there after our move from New York to Washington." For her, an unwanted move that had forced Casey to sell her art gallery—and become, since then, unemployed. "Before the accident, I'd been in the neighborhood after searching for another business site not far from Dupont Circle. I had an appointment near the Mall. And Hearthline." But the question remained: even before the divorce, why didn't her then-husband want her to see his new office?

Now they were divorced and she had to protect herself from a possible killer. She also needed to safeguard her heart from Graham.

If he walked past her once more with that woodsy aroma intermingled with the pheromone-laden scent of man, she might lose her mind. Better to tell him what she could, even when that meant exposing herself.

Casey cleared her throat. "I wanted to drop off the rest of your belongings." She told him about the carton. "You'd left them behind."

His tone sharpened. "Where's the box now?"

"Why, I—" She frowned. To be honest, if she had thought about it during her painful recovery, she'd repressed the memory, like that face in the elevator. "I have no idea," she said lamely, as puzzled as he was.

Graham cruised by the sofa and Casey bit back a moan. "When you woke up, the box was gone?"

"At the hospital, yes. I assumed one of the nurses or someone in Emergency had put it aside for me, but when I was released no one seemed to know anything about the carton. I'm sorry," she added. "Things were chaotic. I hope nothing inside was valuable, sentimental…."

"That's not the point." Graham was clearly losing his patience. "This may be important. What exactly was in that box?"

She tried to relax. Graham too believed that her "accidents" were deliberate, a step forward since yesterday in learning who wanted her dead. She had to do what she could with her now-limited abilities to help catch that killer. Which, right now, meant co-operating with Graham.

"There was a trophy or two—bowling or golf— a few pieces of jewelry you never wore, some toiletries, that kind of thing." *Irish Spring. Aramis.* She paused, wondering if her loss of sight would mean a lifetime of frustrated fantasy. "Are you saying someone ran me down, stole the box—or if not, then entered my apartment to find it? Tried to scare me in the revolving door when he didn't? Why would someone want your stuff?"

"I don't know." He took a deep breath that only seemed, paradoxically, to emit more testosterone into the air. "It's a long shot but we have to consider everything. Maybe this guy is writing a book—*Most Boring Man in the World.* And you had his research."

Casey half laughed but could have groaned. "I wouldn't say that." Graham might be the too-dedicated civil servant with no time for his now-ex-wife, but he'd never bored Casey. All he had to do was walk into a room, and despite her resolve not to, she reacted to his presence.

Like a knife blade of desire, she could sense him with every fiber of her being, hear his familiar footsteps, touch his skin without intending to and feel the heat. But, most especially, she could smell him, his male scent, that tangy aftershave. And almost taste him on her tongue again. Hyperaware, Casey absorbed every shift of his body when he moved. She needed to distract herself.

"There's nothing about your life or mine—the life we shared once—that would appeal to a killer. I sold pretty pictures, Graham." Past tense. "You push papers around on a desk at Hearthline."

She heard him pace some more. "There must be *something* else that triggered those attacks."

When he stopped in front of her, Casey gazed up

at him, wishing she could see even a hint of shadow. She saw nothing, yet she didn't have to. That same, slow burn flared low inside.

Graham had his mind on other things. Real things. Murder, she thought. *Concentrate.*

"If someone wasn't after the box, then what?"

Not long ago, Graham would have soothed her, brushed his finger across her mouth, kissed her until she couldn't breathe. She imagined it now. Hot, dark, compelling…as if he were someone else, that dangerous someone she'd first assumed him to be.

"Come on, Casey. *Think.* From what happened recently, it doesn't seem likely that you went to Hearthline to return my stuff and out of the blue someone decided to whack you. This guy has been tracking you. He pushed you into that revolving door yesterday after letting himself into this apartment. With very few traces left behind, I might add. There's something you haven't told me, or perhaps even remembered…."

That quickly, another memory resurfaced. Casey wanted to send it scurrying back into the far recesses of her mind along with the pain she'd suffered. But that wouldn't help find a potential killer. The words tumbled out.

"I saw a man."

"What man?"

"I don't know. But he may have been coming from Hearthline that day. I watched the indicator drop down from seventeen." Graham's floor. "I was waiting in the lobby with that box for the same elevator to go up. When he stepped out, our gazes met. And locked."

"You knew him. And vice versa."

Casey shook her head. "I'm not sure. I had the odd feeling that I'd met, or seen, him somewhere… maybe some time ago. But I couldn't put a name with his face."

"Why didn't you tell me this before?"

Casey bristled. "Well, for one thing, in the last months of our marriage, you never took that much interest in what I did. You were gone so much that I finally stopped telling you about my days. Why would you care now about my chance meeting with some guy in an elevator?"

"You know why."

She grabbed at straws. "There were other people on the elevator. It stopped at other floors on the way down. Maybe he didn't even get on at Hearthline. He probably has no connection to this whole mess…."

Graham disagreed. "Let me be the judge of that. What did he look like?"

Casey struggled for the image. "Tall, but probably an inch or two less than you. He had blond hair. He wasn't that remarkable, Graham." When she finished her vague description of him and the two men she thought he'd been with, she added, "At least I assumed they were together."

Graham expelled a breath, as if he'd been holding it while she spoke.

"It's not enough. Is it?" she asked when he didn't say a word.

He paced some more. "His face, his clothes, his manner. Nothing stands out." Which seemed to bother Graham.

It didn't trouble Casey. *Please, don't let that stubborn, mind-sticking encounter be significant.* Because if it was, she had looked into the face of the man who might kill her.

"Casey, there must be more."

She briefly shut her eyes, as if to conjure the image again on the blank screen of her lids. Even now, the only picture she could summon of the man remained shadowy. Unlike Graham.

"If he was coming from Hearthline, he could be anyone," she said. "A senator, a journalist, an employee with a job like yours."

"But then, I might recognize him."

Or not, Casey thought. "He could be nobody at all."

"Which is exactly what he may have wanted you to think," Graham murmured in a taut tone.

"You mean, he might hope I would forget him?"

"Right." She heard him rap his knuckles against a tabletop, clearly agitated by her story. "Keep trying to remember where you may have seen him in the past. He could be involved. He could be our man."

Casey worried her lip.

"No, he couldn't be. The time between seeing him at the elevator and my being hit by that car in the garage couldn't have been more than ten minutes."

"Time enough for him to reach the car—and lie in wait for you. Or maybe he called someone else to do the job."

"But *why?*" They kept coming back to that. "Why would someone want to harm me? It doesn't make sense, Graham."

His tone darkened. "Sure it does. If he didn't want you to identify him. He couldn't take the chance on your forgetting him."

"And that reason would be…?"

"I don't know." He crossed the room again and Casey felt him hunker down in front of her. He caught her still-raw hands before she could pull back, and another zing of awareness shot along her veins and nerve endings. "But we'll find out."

We? Casey definitely wouldn't think about that.

She freed her hands. Yet she couldn't hide behind her blindness from reality. Leaning to avoid touching Graham, Casey trailed her hand over Willy's warm, silken fur. He was resting against her leg as if Casey would hold him up. Thanks to Graham, she had the dog now to protect her. Yet he wasn't all she would need to find a killer, no matter what the reason for the attacks might be.

Whether or not she liked the fact, Casey also needed Graham. Willy would be her guide. But Graham would have to be her eyes.

AN HOUR LATER, from his car in the same parking garage where Casey had been hit, Graham punched in numbers on his cell phone, then waited for his contact at the D.C. police department to answer. The job was relatively new for Holt Kincade, but he had a lot of other experience.

Not long ago, he'd been deep-cover like Graham.

"Hey, Holt. How's life back in the world?"

A soft Southern drawl came over the line. "Not bad. You still building that government pension?"

Graham didn't need to answer. From Holt, the question would be rhetorical. Quickly, he explained about Casey's initial accident. "I need to get my hands on the police report."

After supplying the necessary details that would access Casey's file, he waited, drumming his fingers against the steering wheel. He didn't like what Casey had told him, but he wasn't getting anywhere. He'd already looked around the parking garage himself without finding any clues.

"She mentioned three men in the elevator, possibly coming from the seventeenth floor at Hearthline," he said to Holt. "One of whom may have recognized her. But from where, when? And why were those men there at all?" Graham felt in his gut that they didn't belong.

"Something's not right," Holt agreed.

"I'll have to check the visitors' log." Because of the need for tight security at the agency, it was kept religiously. Would three names show up on that log after normal business hours? Graham couldn't shake the feeling that Casey's first accident and at least one of those men were connected.

"Here we go," Holt said. "I've pulled it up on my computer screen. The report is pretty cut and dried. No eye witnesses at the scene except your ex, and she was either out cold on the floor of that garage or she was drifting in and out of consciousness until the next day," Holt said. "There's not even a good description here of the car that hit her."

"It would help if we had a license plate number or at least the make and model of the car, its color."

"A few paint chips wouldn't hurt," Holt agreed. "From the impact of the accident, we might be able to link them to a fiber from the clothes she was wearing at the time, or maybe a strand of her hair caught in the paint. All she could tell the cops who interviewed her was that the car was a sedan—she thought—and dark."

Graham sighed. "That covers a lot of territory. Probably half the cars in D.C." The nation's capital had no shortage of plain dark sedans, not to mention town cars and limos.

Knowing, too, that they were a dime a dozen, Holt made a sound of frustration that matched Gra-

ham's mood. "Well, the car did come at her from behind." Another computer key clicked, probably to
scroll down on his screen. "She apparently didn't see
the driver, male or female. Neither did anyone else,
as far as I know."

"All of that jibes with the scant details Casey gave
me." Graham asked about the missing box she had
carried. He couldn't discount any possibility. Had her
attacker really been after Graham?

"Nope. Nothing here on any box. You might dou-
ble-check with the hospital. They'd have any belongings left behind except for the clothes she was
wearing at the time of the accident. We kept those
for evidence."

"The ambulance guys might know something."
The box might prove nothing, but Casey had been
run down near his office building, and Graham didn't
believe in coincidences. Either the box was part of
the problem, or Casey had indeed seen something—
or someone—she shouldn't have seen.

"Want me to fax you a copy of the report?"

"Yeah. At home. Thanks, Holt. I owe you one."

"Don't mention it. I'll never be able to repay my
debt to you." Graham winced. On one dark-as-hell
night in Beirut, he had saved Holt's life, but Graham
shrugged that off. He knew Holt would do the same
for him. "Wish I could be more help," he added.

"Wait. Maybe you can." Graham straightened in
his seat. He told Holt about Casey's second mishap

in the revolving door the day before. He tapped the steering wheel again while Holt scrambled through the most recent police write-ups—and found nothing.

Graham cursed himself. "I should have gotten the name of the guy who was almost hit when Casey's assailant tore out of that parking space. His SUV did get bumped pretty hard. Maybe he didn't file a report to keep his insurance rate from rising. I guess I was too concerned about Casey to think straight at the time."

"No wonder." Holt paused. His voice deepened and his Tennessee accent intensified, a sure sign he was troubled. "By the way, I was real sorry to hear about Casey's eyes. That's a tough one, Graham. How's she dealin' with it?"

"Better than could be expected."

Holt hesitated again. "You two getting back together?"

"Not as far as I know," Graham repeated Holt's earlier phrase. Graham had a job to do. That was all.

At least that's what he kept trying to tell himself. For her own safety, Casey had to keep thinking, like almost everyone else at Hearthline, that he was some dull civil servant in a dead-end job. A guy who hadn't cared enough about her to stay home at night. Until this was over, he'd keep quiet—if it killed *him.*

Casey was already at risk.

The less she knew about Graham's real work, the

better. For now. As an ex-operative, Holt would understand.

"I hope you find what you're lookin' for, partner."

The term was more than a throwaway word. Holt Kincade had been on the twelve-member team with Graham when the original antiterrorism task force began. He and Graham and Tom Dallas.

"So do I."

Graham wondered whether Holt meant the rest of the story, the possible killer or Casey herself.

CASEY'S HEART pounded. All around her, horns blew. Five o'clock traffic rushed past. "We can do this," she told herself and Willy.

Graham, who had late meetings to attend, had dropped them off at the Guide Dog Institute on his way back to work, saying his colleague, Jackie Miles, would pick her up. She was not to leave until Jackie got there.

Like the memory of Graham's face and body, their earlier conversation still hummed in Casey's mind. But she couldn't afford second thoughts. Casey had been unable to sit home and do nothing—as Graham might prefer. This little trip had seemed harmless, even necessary at the time, in order to maintain her independence. Now they had to get home—their first solo trip—and Willy waited patiently beside her on the corner near the institute.

Why hadn't Jackie Miles kept her promise to meet

Casey? She had waited in the reception office for over an hour. But still no Jackie. Weeks ago the woman had kindly spent time with Casey at the hospital whenever Graham couldn't be there, sitting by her bed, chatting with Casey when she woke. Why hadn't she shown up this time?

Casey took a deep breath. With rush hour peaking by the minute in downtown D.C., how likely could it be that another car would run her down, in broad daylight on a busy street just blocks from the Mall, the White House, the FBI? Even Hearthline?

Unlikely, she decided. Besides, what choice did she have? When she'd phoned Graham, his cell phone had been busy. Neither Rafe Valera—forbidden territory—nor Anton had been home. She didn't know anyone else in D.C. to call about a ride.

"Forward, Willy."

In one hand she grasped the dog's harness and felt him dutifully take a step. Then another, always ready to sense if she felt okay about the next one before he guided her onward.

Leaving the curb they crossed the street, then moved down the opposite sidewalk. Casey relaxed a little. Willy was a real pro. Already, she couldn't remember what she'd done without him.

After their lesson at the institute, she felt proud of the small progress they'd made. Casey walked with a new confidence down the bustling street toward the nearby Metro entrance.

She could do this, but she couldn't take a cab, the more sensible, perhaps safer, alternative. Let Graham grumble. She didn't have enough money for a taxi, hadn't expected to need it.

The afternoon breeze, hot and humid, blew across her face, and Casey lifted her gaze to the still-blazing sun. She didn't need to try so hard, her teacher had said. She needed to trust her dog not only to get her across the street but, Casey knew, to keep her safe.

Odd, for some reason that seemed easier than leaning on Graham even when she had to. But then, the beautiful golden retriever had never hurt her. Casey hadn't forgotten the long evenings at home alone while Graham worked endlessly. The even longer weeks when he'd been on the road to somewhere, his painful absences, their dwindling conversations when he was home, her empty bed more nights than not.

At one point she'd assumed—wrongly, Graham insisted—that he was having an affair. In the end, even their less frequent sex hadn't mattered. Finally, Casey had made the tough decision to save herself.

At the next corner Willy stopped and she halted beside him, she assumed, for a red light.

"Good boy," she said. "We worked hard today."

The traffic light clicked green, and Willy stepped out again. His nails tapped on the street, then a minute later up onto the sidewalk.

They were coming up the very long, steeply graded escalator typical of the Washington Metro ten minutes later when Casey went on full-alert. So did Willy, her "point man," just in front of her. Surrounded by people on their way home from work, she sensed the instant someone else was there at her shoulder on the moving step behind her. Someone who didn't belong. Casey didn't know how she knew. She just did.

Her pulse thudded, fast.

They were definitely being watched.

Worse, they had been followed.

Casey could feel the pull at Willy's harness that meant he had turned his head to look at her. He felt her tension.

Is everything okay? he seemed to ask.

"No," she whispered. "It's not."

On the crowded escalator that slowly inched its way upward from the Metro tunnel toward the light, and the street, there was nowhere to go. She heard people talking. Inhaled the heavy, turgid air of the subway. Felt the sweaty handrail beneath her fingers. Weeks ago, she would have charged her way through the crowd. Now she couldn't move. She couldn't breathe. She couldn't *see*.

A punishing hand clamped down on her shoulder. And Casey froze. Her heart went wild. His sleeve brushed against her bare arm, the fabric feeling silky, expensive. She could smell a hint of musky cologne, clean and spicy. Familiar. She would have given anything for the man to be Graham. But he wasn't.

She heard Willy growl. Quick and full of menace. Like the man's hard voice.

"I'm telling you, bitch. You didn't see a thing."

"Who are—?"

"Just get this straight." He snarled in her ear. "'Hear no evil. *See* no evil. Speak no evil.' You open that pretty mouth and you'll wish your bad eyesight was the only problem you have. Next time, you're *dead*."

At that instant, as if he had timed it, the escalator reached street level. People piled off and so did her assailant.

She would never forget him. She knew him by his scent. *The man in the elevator!*

Casey's pulse hammered. *It doesn't make sense. Sure it does. If he didn't want you to identify him.*

Did he know she'd talked to Graham? But how? And who was he? She couldn't *remember*.

Willy was still growling deep in his throat.

His nails scraped against the pavement, scrabbling for purchase, and he lunged against his harness, as if to tear after the man. She pulled sharply on his handle to keep him beside her.

"It's all right, Willy." Her voice quavered.

Casey's first steps felt jerky. Determined not to panic, she held on tight to Willy's harness as he threaded his way through the throng of rush-hour pedestrians. Yet she could feel his tension too, vibrating through the leather harness into her hand, then along her arm to her rigid shoulder where the phantom grasp of her attacker's hand still burned.

First, she'd been run down. Then had come the whirling disorientation in the revolving doors. And the break-in that wasn't really a break-in.

Now, she couldn't deny the threat that had been uttered, low and harsh, in her ear. *Speak no evil.*

Trembling, her pulse beating like one of the Japanese Taiko drums from a performance she'd once arranged at her gallery, Casey urged the dog to a faster pace. Not toward home. Down the escalator. Into the Metro. To the platform again. She didn't want to plunge back into the darkness—yet it was always there now, inside her.

She didn't go home. Instead, Casey headed back downtown to Hearthline.

Despite his best effort, Sweet William wasn't enough to protect her. Casey feared nothing would be.

Chapter Four

"May I help you?"

A cool British-accented voice spoke from the nearby receptionist's desk at Hearthline. Casey gave Willy the signal to move, and they walked closer.

Her short journey from the Metro had seemed to take forever. She suspected it would be much longer before she stopped hearing that other, menacing dark voice in her ear.

Next time you're dead.

If only Willy could have protected her from those vicious words.

If only Casey could have *seen* the man's face....

Still, she had heard his voice. Clearly.

And she could identify him now by his smell, one reason for her surprise visit to Graham's office.

Casey hesitated. She didn't imagine he'd be pleased, but she needed to tell him what had happened. What if the assailant, the same man she'd seen before in the elevator, worked in this building?

Her heart beat faster.

How would she find Graham?

She'd never made it farther than this the last time. The night security guard had blocked her path. And when Casey asked for Graham, he gave her a blank look. Was the guard new on the job?

Casey had wanted, badly, to slip past him. But she'd had no choice. After thanking the guard, who by then seemed suspicious of her, she'd turned and, taking the box of Graham's things with her, had left.

Moments later, she'd been lying on the concrete floor of the parking garage, battered and blind.

Now Casey sucked in a breath.

"I'd like to see Gr—"

"I'll need your security pass, ma'am."

Or you will be escorted from this building.

Casey could imagine the frigid-voiced receptionist discreetly pushing some button to summon the guard.

"Oh, my. What a surprise." Casey turned at the sound of a bright female voice, which sounded familiar. She sensed the newcomer bending down to scratch Willy's ears.

Willy growled again. "Be careful," Casey said. "He's wary of strangers."

"He must be angry with me. You, too," she said and Casey recognized the other voice. Jackie Miles, Graham's co-worker. Jackie had stood her up at the Guide Dog Institute and she hastened to apologize.

Jackie's voice sounded uncertain. "I'm so sorry.

I know I was supposed to meet you, but I got tied up here...."

Her lame explanation didn't ring true. It appeared Jackie hadn't even left Hearthline with the intention of taking Casey home.

But why not?

GRAHAM LEANED BACK in his office chair and swore. This was what he'd expected. He didn't have to like it, though. He scowled into the phone.

"So there were no identifiable prints in Casey's apartment?"

Holt's drawl was already under full sail. "There were plenty of prints. Hers, yours, Valera's and his son's. That's it."

"What about the partial you mentioned?"

"Smeared," Holt said. "May not be enough to go on. We'll keep working on it."

"It does prove that someone else was there."

"Maybe. A telephone repairman, the building super, some kid who delivers her groceries."

"But that's not what you really think."

Holt sighed, apparently frustrated, too. "What I think is, this guy is slick. Experienced, like you said. If I don't miss my personal guess, he wiped that apartment clean before he left. And made sure he didn't touch very much in the first place. We found that partial on Casey's answering machine."

Holt rustled through some papers.

"I did find a report that may interest you."

Graham sensed his smile bloom across the wires, and felt as if he was about to explode with anticipation. "Listen to this. Your pal, the one who nearly got cut down when the guy escaped after spinnin' Casey in that door?"

Graham's pulse sped. "Yeah?"

"After you and I spoke last time, he came in. Filed a report on the incident." Holt said. "His insurance company insisted upon it, but the guy is hoppin' mad, too. He bought that SUV only the day before and now it's in the body shop."

"He give a good description of the perp?"

"Depends on how you look at it."

Graham sighed. True to his Southern roots, Holt got to the point in his own good time.

"Dark hair. Dark eyes. Dark suit. Sound familiar?"

"Sure fits my description of him." And classic. Unremarkable, like Casey's man in the elevator. Only different.

A bad sign. His skin crawled.

"Maybe we can put together a sketch. Can you get the victim to come in again?"

"Chances may be good. He was pretty steamed." Holt paused, having, as usual, saved the punch line for last. "Oh, and there's one more thing. This you'll really like."

CASEY HAD ALMOST expected the other shoe to drop.

"Jackie." The receptionist's icy voice stopped

them halfway down the hall. "Your friend will need to sign in."

"I'll do it for her." Jackie's tone was a reproach. It would be clear to anyone that Casey couldn't sign for herself. "Wait here," she told Casey.

When she rejoined her, Jackie muttered, "Bureaucracy. You just saw—sorry, I mean, *caught*—that in action." She guided Casey down the remaining length of the hall.

On either side as they passed, Casey could hear computer keys clicking, men and women talking in hushed tones or on the telephone, and at one office a television set was blaring the latest news. Casey had the odd impression that Jackie was hustling her along, and she didn't seem to invite further conversation.

Casey took a sniff as they went by each office. This might be her one chance to find the man who'd accosted her in the subway but so far she'd come up empty. And, she was sure, so had Willy. He was very much into smells, and she doubted he would forget that scent soon, either.

Casey inhaled the fast-food hangover in the air, the smell of onions and grease, burnt coffee, then a mingling of perfumes and aftershaves. But none of them belonged to the man who had threatened her.

At the next door Jackie stopped. She tapped her nails against the frame for attention.

"Come on in," Casey heard Graham say in a distracted tone, probably with his back still to the door.

Computer keys clacked in that nonstop rhythm Graham used whenever he was deep into a "project." Casey didn't care right now. Although muffled, his deep voice flowed over her like a comforting blanket, warming the blood in her veins. She inhaled his unique, clean male scent, and she felt her whole body sag in relief. Never mind his order to stay away from Hearthline. She was here. He was here. It would be okay now. *She* would be okay.

The thought astonished her.

Until that moment Casey hadn't realized how shattered she felt from the incident on the Metro escalator. How much she still relied on Graham.

"I brought you a visitor," Jackie said.

And the keys stopped clicking. Graham spun around. Casey heard his chair squeak. In the next instant he was on his feet, at the door, hauling her inside. "What are you doing here?"

"Hello to you, too," Casey murmured, feeling more and more puzzled by his new environment, Graham's place in it and his attitude.

"I thought you were driving her home," he said to Jackie.

"We had a change of plan—"

Graham cut her off. "Jackie, give us a minute alone."

"Sure," she said. "I took care of things out front. Want me to close your door?"

"Please." As soon as Jackie was gone, Graham dragged a chair close and guided Casey to it. "Sit," he said.

She heard him lean down to pet Willy, who had immediately flopped at her feet. Willy wiggled his whole body in delight at the affection from his friend. He adored Graham.

"I thought I *told* you—"

"Never to come here." Casey swallowed. His voice sounded angry, more so than she'd expected. So much for the brief solace she'd just enjoyed. "Yes. I know. But Graham, something happened."

His tone sharpened. "What?"

Casey told him about Jackie's failure to meet her, and about the man in the subway. After he calmed down, Graham told her about the fingerprint, then described her revolving-door assailant.

"What is going on here?" She meant Hearthline, too.

"Nothing." She could tell he was lying. Casey knew him too well. "I'll deal with Jackie. Are you okay?" he said.

"Yes."

"Did you call the police?"

"No. He disappeared into the crowd. I wasn't hurt. What would I tell them?"

"Right." The single word seemed to question her judgment. "So then, even though you were a few blocks from home, you decided to come back here."

"Because I hoped to find him at Hearthline." *Because I needed to find you.* "Your cell phone was busy. Rafe and Anton weren't home. I didn't want to risk going there alone. Graham, I could *smell* him. Right here in this building the day I was hit. Then today, again, on that escalator. Don't you see? I'm sure it was the same man."

"Because you detected the same cologne or soap," Graham mused.

Casey nodded her head. "It's not a scent I ever smelled before. Maybe it's a special aftershave. Personally blended for him. That's good, isn't it? We can trace that." Now that she felt safe, she let excitement take over. "It could be evidence. And he may be someone important. His suit was expensive, I could tell just by looking at it in the elevator that day."

By habit Casey noticed clothes, colors, shapes. Or she had when she'd owned her gallery.

"But you can't remember his face."

"I can't *place* the face," she corrected Graham.

"Well, we'll try to do something about that." He told her that he and the innocent bystander whose car had been hit would try to form a composite picture of her assailant via a police artist. "Maybe our description will help trigger some memory for you. Some place where you saw this guy before."

"How, when I won't be able to see the sketch?" Then Casey sat straighter in her chair and her face paled. "Graham, you said the man in the revolving door was dark. The man I *saw* that first day wasn't. He was fair."

"You only smelled his scent then—and on the escalator today? Not at the doctor's building or in your apartment?"

Casey shook her head. She stared blankly down at her hands, folded on her lap.

"I was afraid of that. The thought occurred to me earlier." She heard him sigh. "We're dealing with more than one guy."

"Which makes it even worse," she guessed.

"Or better. Bigger, anyway." His voice brightened. "In this case, there's no safety in numbers. More chances for somebody to make a mistake. And speaking of numbers…"

Graham dropped back into his desk chair, taking his broad shoulders, his heat, his masculine scent with him. Casey heard the snap of computer keys again. Was he returning to his own work? Dismissing her? Then she knew she was wrong. Right now his work concerned *her*. Graham spoke as he typed.

"When Holt Kincade—he's with the Washington police—told me about the report on the damaged SUV, he also said the driver had gotten a partial license plate number for the other car. It led nowhere. But I wonder…"

More keys flew.

Casey waited, patting Willy to soothe herself, sensing the change of mood.

"Ha," he said after another moment. He rattled off the numbers reported by the SUV owner. "What if this guy is dyslexic?" Graham hypothesized. "Then he might reverse a few numbers. I'll plug what he gave us into the computer and let it work through some possibilities." A few seconds later, he let out a soft whistle. "Oh, yeah. I'm sending this to Holt."

They didn't have to wait for long.

Within minutes Graham's phone rang. Casey couldn't hear the other end of the conversation, but from his reactions, and the new charge of excitement that emanated from Graham, Casey hoped it was good news.

Graham hung up. He shoved his seat back, then stood, those sharp waves of energy rolling off his body to fill the room with electricity. A second later he was standing in front of her. Casey didn't get the chance to ask what had happened. Before she knew it, Graham pulled her up from her seat and into his arms. Then, to her utter astonishment, while she was still trying not to welcome that strong embrace, he lowered his head and his mouth crushed hers in a hard, surprising kiss.

The first in many long months.

The room spun, as if she'd been thrust again into that revolving door. His male scent drifted through the air, and his lips were warm, sexy. Casey heard her own breath catch. Another instant and she'd be clinging to him. Forgetting their divorce. Forgetting all about the man on the escalator and the terror she'd felt.

Instead, Graham quickly pulled back.

"Babe, we just got lucky." As if the kiss didn't affect him at all, he put on his suit jacket, then led her and Willy to the door. "Holt found a match with those numbers I e-mailed him, a dark sedan like the one that hit you—and an owner's registration through the Department of Motor Vehicles. We're meeting him at that address. Let's get out of here."

"DO YOU HAVE to drive so fast?"

She was right. Graham always drove fast, but he was setting a record now, especially for rush-hour traffic. Weaving in and out, he headed for the address Holt had given him.

If nothing more, Graham would see Casey's assailant in jail tonight.

If he got really lucky, they might also break the case on which he'd been working—and if a miracle occurred, find a clue to that security leak. He couldn't shake the feeling now that the two were connected, the terrorist plot and Casey's attacks.

The man she had seen in the elevator at Hearthline could be the one Graham wanted. A traitor who was selling secrets to Al-Hassan. The thought made him light-headed.

"You're making me dizzy," Casey tried again.

"Sorry. You okay?"

"If I say, 'never better,' will you believe me?"

Graham half smiled. She still had her sense of humor after all. Her spirit. Yet he knew she also had her suspicions. About him.

That was his fault, too.

He could kill Jackie Miles for screwing up.

By necessity, he hadn't wanted to risk Casey running into his superiors at Hearthline, having one of them call Graham by the wrong name. DeLucci had eyes like a hawk. When they left the office, Graham had checked the hallway to make sure it was clear. Then, with his heart still thundering in his chest after that explosive kiss he and Casey had shared, he urged her and Willy into the fire exit stairwell. He prayed she wouldn't demand some explanation, but using the steps meant avoiding the reception desk and anyone waiting for, or getting off, the elevators.

Of course, maybe it didn't matter now.

Had his cover already been blown? he wondered again.

So far it didn't seem so but he wasn't sure.

If it wasn't for Jackie whisking Casey into his office and out of sight when she arrived, it would be amazing if it hadn't been blown. If someone *had* recognized Casey near his office that first day, before her accident, he might well ID her now, too.

Graham wasn't taking any chances.

"Seventeen flights?" Casey had murmured from the step above him on their way down. "Why is it necessary for me to have a heart attack? What good will I be to you then? And poor Willy."

The clasp of her hand in his as he led her down the stairs set Graham's pulse running harder, faster, than even that fleeting touch of her lips to his. Oh, man. He had no right to that one forbidden kiss, but if he died right now, he'd die a happy man.

It was only sexual attraction, he told himself, and having once been married to her only made that worse. He had all those memories of kisses in the dark, the feel of her body, her skin... Graham supposed that by tonight, even with Casey's attacker in jail, he'd get no sleep. He had a hard enough task putting her out of his mind every other night. Now he had today's kiss to remember. And remember...

Graham cleared his throat. He needed to block out everything except keeping Casey safe and exposing the truth.

"Graham, please. Slow down."

He eased off on the accelerator. Her blindness must play havoc with her sense of balance, and his attempt to turn Wisconsin Avenue into a NASCAR track was probably making her feel a whole lot sicker than she let on.

"I'm a jerk," he said.

"But a very charming jerk."

Only her voice didn't sound judgmental. It sounded soft, husky, laced with humor and full of the same new memory he had. Damn.

"I hope you don't get another ticket," she added.

"We're almost there."

Because it matched his own, he could sense her growing excitement. Which triggered another spurt of anger at her assailants. What would it mean to Casey to have her life back again? To focus her efforts on coping with her blindness and moving again toward some happier place?

A place without him.

So maybe she hadn't felt the same heat from that kiss. Graham ran a hand over his five o'clock stubble. He had given her a bad time, he and his oh-so-important job for the U.S. government.

She deserved happiness. With someone else.

"Hell." Graham pulled up in front of the address Holt had given him, but he saw no other cars around. The driveway was empty. The modest frame house and scrubby yard looked deserted. There were no cruisers out front. "The cops are late."

"They don't have your traffic skills."

"Yeah, yeah." But he offered her a smile. A smile Casey couldn't see.

Instead, he took her hand. "Why don't you wait here? I'll take a look, see if I can spot that dark sedan."

"No way. I'm coming, too."

Casey pulled her hand free, opened the passenger door and got out. She released Willy from his bed on the rear seat and grabbed on to his harness.

Graham sighed as he joined her on the sidewalk. At his first step he froze.

The air around him took on that heavy, overbearing feel that prickled his neck. Like the instant before someone pushed Casey into that revolving door.

"Casey, I want you to stay here."

She kept going. "It was *my* accident. I've spent the past few weeks in fear of my own shadow. If the guy who owns that car lives here and he's linked to the man I saw in the elevator and the man on the escalator, I want to hear the cuffs snap into place."

Graham caught her shoulder. "Later. Right now there's something wrong."

She sent him a quizzical look. Willy did, too.

Electricity seemed to zing through the atmosphere into Graham's body, along his nerve endings. Either he needed a vacation, or they were walking into trouble.

At the garage door he peered inside, holding Casey back with one hand on her forearm. He could feel her pulse beat, too, under his fingers. Quick and strong.

"Do you see the car?"

"No."

But then he changed his mind. He saw *something*. Something bad?

"Please. Wait here."

He left her standing with Willy, looking after Graham with a puzzled expression. Better she should feel confused than get hurt again.

Adrenaline pumping, he slipped into the garage through the side door. Not to his surprise, it had been unlocked.

A second later he was crouching over a woman lying in the interior doorway, half in the garage, half inside the adjoining kitchen.

At a slight sound behind him, Graham automatically reached for his gun, hidden by his sports jacket in his shoulder holster. He drew it out only to find Casey at the side entrance, her head tilted with curiosity in his direction.

"Graham?"

"There's a woman here," he told her. When he hunkered down, her hand fell open and he saw something else that made fresh alarm rush through him. "She's dead."

Chapter Five

Casey inhaled the unmistakable, metallic scent of blood. Lots of it, if her nose was giving her an accurate assessment.

The smell seemed to permeate the oxygen around her, sucking it dry and turning her stomach. She held one hand in front of her, palming the air, feeling her way with Willy at her side so she wouldn't bump into things. She inched forward from the doorway, but she didn't know exactly where Graham might be. And anyone's garage was rarely a neat place. People left all sorts of things lying around to trap the unwary.

Including, it seemed, a dead body.

Casey shivered. Willy whined and tried to back away.

Graham's voice cut through the still air. "Willy, down. Stay there, Casey."

"Graham?" she said again.

Her heart thudded, but she forced herself to take

another step. She didn't want to be alone. Excluded by her blindness. Vulnerable in this place of death. The murderer could still be here. What if he was lurking behind a garbage can? Or in an adjacent workshop? Surprised after committing his heinous crime, he might attack again.

She heard Graham swiftly cross the space between them, then felt him grasp her shoulders. Casey's skin tingled at the contact.

"Go outside." He led her to the door again, then pushed it open, herding Willy right with her. "Stand here, on the sidewalk." His tone was grim. "The police should have turned up by now. I'll give 911 and Holt another call."

He had started to use his cell phone when a soft shriek of brakes at the nearby curb informed them that the cops were, indeed, here now. Casey heard doors slamming, and the low buzz of men's voices.

Gasping for fresh air, she inhaled it, along with the welcome scent of summer flowers. Marigolds, she thought. Sharp and pungent, the foliage cleansed her nostrils after the stench of death inside the garage.

In the utter stillness, she sensed the presence of a soul—that of a woman who'd been cut off in the prime of life.

Who had she been?

Why was she killed?

And—the question uppermost in Casey's mind—

what did it have to do with her own "accident" with the dark sedan that had belonged to someone who presumably lived here? Its owner had apparently vanished.

There were worse things, Casey told herself, than being blind.

FOR THE FIRST TIME, Graham appreciated Casey's blindness. He didn't want her to see this.

He stood with Holt Kincade off to one side while the rest of the cops practiced crowd control with the curiosity seekers who kept drifting by the house. Holt reread his notes. They weren't much, but they did provide a starting place.

"Marilee Baxter. Thirty-five years old. Single. Rented this place about six months ago. According to the landlord, her name's the only one on the lease." Holt slapped his notebook shut. "He also says she and the guy were livin' together. Guess her old man was really pissed about something."

Graham glanced toward Casey, now waiting in his car. From her first reaction, standing pale and wide-eyed in the doorway to the garage, he could tell she was shaken.

Hell, so was he.

It wasn't the first time Graham had seen death, but it never got easier to deal with. On a battlefield, or at the site of a raid on a terrorist cell, even once during training when a new recruit had fatally shot himself by accident… Graham didn't go on with the mental list. It had always been hard to swallow the bitter bile that rose in his throat.

Holt ran a hand over his military-short blond hair. "What the hell did that woman do to deserve such a brutal end?"

Good question. "Nasty business. Looks like the work of a garrote," Graham muttered.

"Cut right through her carotid artery. She didn't have a chance. Bled out in minutes." Holt caught himself. "But we'll wait for the autopsy for the official cause of death."

Behind them, the overhead garage door cranked open on its automatic rollers. Graham averted his eyes when the medics carried the victim, packaged neatly in a black body bag, past them to the waiting ambulance. So did Holt, shielding his expression with hooded eyes.

"I can't find much info on the guy who owns that dark sedan," Holt said, shrugging his wide shoulders. "Beyond his registration and insurance, *de nada*. Probably a false ID. I've got an all-points out, but he could be halfway to Florida by now. Let's hope he has a bad taillight or a heavy foot on the gas. Some highway patrolman might pull him over and take note." He eyed Graham with suspicion. "You didn't touch anything in there?" He gestured at the garage.

Technicians carrying bags of evidence walked by

with crisp nods for Holt, then Graham, and hurried to their van.

"Nope. Didn't disturb the scene. I was too busy watching out for Casey."

"You sure?"

Another of Holt's double entendres. Was Graham sure of what? Taking care of his ex-wife, who tolerated his help only in times of high stress and desperation? Or sure that he hadn't taken valuable evidence for his own purposes? Graham wouldn't answer.

He studied the yellow crime scene tape around the perimeter of the yard. He watched a mother herd her teenage kid back across the street, her fingers pinching his ear to keep him walking.

If Graham couldn't convince the shrewd cop that he was innocent, he would be facing an obstruction of justice charge, not a crowd of onlookers craning their necks for another glimpse of mayhem.

But how could *he,* in good conscience, withhold evidence in this case? That was easy. And very personal.

When he'd found the cuff link that had been clutched in Marilee Baxter's hand, it all but struck him right between the eyes.

Graham shook off his troubling thoughts when he spied the media news van rolling down the street toward the victim's house.

"I'd better go. I need to get Casey home."

The two men strolled toward the curb. Better than

most people, Holt would appreciate the fact that Graham didn't want his face on the evening news, which only made him feel more guilty for his deception.

But Holt didn't need to know about the small item now wrapped in Graham's handkerchief and buried deep in his pant pocket.

He shot another look at Casey. Like Willy, her head was turned his way. For an instant, he imagined their gazes met and locked. As if she knew what he'd done. The dog, too.

For a government operative who worked undercover most of the time, Graham was a damn bad liar in his personal life. No wonder she'd never believed him.

"That's it, then." Holt headed for his squad car. "I'll let you know what we turn up. You do the same, hear?"

Guilt dragged his steps as Graham lifted a hand then walked to his own car, relieved he couldn't see Holt's suspicious gaze. Casey was still staring out the window at him. Asking him for the truth.

He couldn't give it to her. A woman was dead. The stakes had risen and he had a killer to catch.

Now Graham also had evidence. He would use it but in his own way. If he wasn't mistaken, national security was also at risk. The key, so to speak, just might be in his pocket.

Graham was scowling when he opened his door. He had lied to Holt. He knew he couldn't lie—

wouldn't this time—to Casey. She had a right to know at least part of the truth, assuming it could help their case.

SAFE IN HER living room, Casey held the small gold cuff link in her palm, which was covered by Graham's handkerchief. She started to trace a finger over its unusual shape then along the narrow shaft of its fastener. She couldn't get the dead woman—Marilee Baxter—out of her mind.

"Don't unwrap it!" Graham ordered. "I'll tell you what it looks like. Ruby, sapphire, diamond chips in a gold star." She could hear the sharpness but also the grimace in his tone. He disliked male jewelry to begin with. Cufflinks, chains, bracelets weren't Graham's thing. In fact, he preferred a plain, unvarnished appearance. The only time she'd known him to wear jewelry at all had been his wedding band. Sometimes she'd wondered if he'd even worn that when he was away from home.

"Not too flashy, although it sounds it," he went on in a hopeful note, which surprised her. "Unique," he added as if to prompt her.

Then he waited.

For her reaction, she realized.

Casey ran her finger over the gem-encrusted metal through the cloth. Near her feet Willy dozed, making small snuffling noises in his sleep. A comforting sound. But Casey couldn't relax.

"Red, white and blue. The colors of the U.S. flag," she said. Suddenly her back straightened on the sofa.

"Bingo."

"Graham, your team leader gave you a pair of cuff links after the Houston bombing of the Federal court building, didn't he? When you went with the task force from—" She couldn't remember which job he'd held then.

"HUD."

"Housing and Urban Development. I remember you were gone for three weeks that time, helping to clean up the debris, settle claims in the surrounding neighborhood, arrange loans for rebuilding." It wasn't the last time.

"Good memory." He added, "He gave a pair to every member of that team. A dozen in all."

"You never wore yours." But she recalled him showing the cuff links to her. Proudly.

"Hey. I'm not a party animal," he said. Graham led a very quiet life, or he had until recently. For which he had Casey to blame.

"I've changed all that. One minute you were shoving papers around on your desk at Hearthline, the next you're protecting your ex-wife from a killer. I feel terrible for involving you."

She also had her suspicions. Of him.

"Don't worry about me," he said.

Casey felt him kneel in front of her. When he took her hands, and his harder male flesh touched her softer skin, she forgot her own questions. A flash of need whipped through her, but she realized she was still trembling. No matter how tightly she gripped herself, she couldn't stop remembering those minutes in that garage with Marilee Baxter lying dead nearby.

What had her last moments been like?

Did she die quickly, slowly? Mercifully or in pain?

If he knew, Graham wouldn't share the details. "It was fatal all right," was all he'd said.

Part of her didn't want to know more than that. The rest of her felt like those neighbors murmuring outside the Blazer, crowding close to the crime-scene tape, pressing against Graham's SUV where Casey had sat, still smelling blood.

Now he unclasped her fingers, removed the warmed cuff link from her grasp, and she knew.

"It was in her hand. Wasn't it?" Casey asked.

Marilee Baxter had been holding the cuff link when she died.

"Yeah."

"Which means the person who murdered her probably owned a pair of these cuff links."

"Right," he said. "I think we can assume that."

Casey shivered. "And now one of them is missing. What did Detective Kincade say?"

Graham hesitated. "He, uh, didn't."

"He doesn't know?" Casey said, astonished. "But that's—"

"Yeah. I'm guilty as hell. You and Willy can visit me in jail."

"But why—?"

"You know why. If I turn this over to Holt, we'll never see it again. It'll get buried in the evidence locker until the murder trial, perhaps years from now. We need this cuff link, Casey. There were twelve pairs," he repeated. "Twelve men."

Casey realized where he was going. "Eleven," she murmured, "besides you. You think one of them killed the woman in the garage. One of them is the guy whose registration for a dark sedan led us to that house. The same man who is trying to kill me."

"That's what we're going to find out."

"His registration—you don't recognize his name?"

"No. It sounds familiar but I can't pin it down, just like you and the guy you saw in the elevator." Graham blew out a breath. "Now one of those twelve men is missing a single cuff link. When we find him, we'll find the twin from the same pair."

"Unless he gave away the cuff links after Houston, or pawned them. Then they could belong to anyone."

"I doubt that. They were a memento for our service there. Government-issue they were not. Our team leader had those cuff links designed and made. So obviously, one guy is going around now under an assumed name."

And C.A.T., the newer group to which he belonged, wanted to talk to him. Graham stroked one finger across the back of her hand. His rougher skin cruised over her softer flesh again and Casey felt that slow burn flare inside her.

"Graham."

"The man in the elevator. Casey, try to remember something about him other than his smell. A name would really help."

When Casey came up with nothing, she could feel Graham's disappointment. It dovetailed with her own.

"It's okay. We'll keep trying. First," he said, "I'll find all the other men and interview them."

Graham lifted his hand to brush her cheek, then let his fingers slide lower to cradle her chin. That slow wave of desire rolled deeper within her body. Graham's voice was a soft murmur, like the light caress against her cheek.

"I'm sorry about today. You'd already been through enough."

For a moment she could sense him staring at her mouth. Casey licked her dry lips, and heard Graham suck in a hard breath. When he spoke, his tone had turned hoarse.

"Stick close, babe. Marilee Baxter—the cuff link—the dark sedan and the phony registration… they're all part of the same thing."

"The reason someone wants to kill me."

His next words made her breath catch.

"Yes," he agreed. "That, and possibly a hell of a lot more."

Chapter Six

One of those twelve men had turned traitor.

Graham hadn't mentioned that to Casey. For her own good, she didn't need to know.

But the real question was: Which man?

Had Marilee Baxter been murdered to shut her up? Would whoever the killer was stop next time with warning Casey?

Graham ordered himself to stay cool when he and Jackie Miles entered the well-appointed living room where the first of his ex-teammates now lived. That original task force had been scuttled after 9/11, to be replaced by C.A.T., on which Graham now served along with Jackie.

"David Wells. We meet again." He shook hands with the other man but Graham had never liked him much. For one thing, he lived too well. This big house in the Maryland suburbs reeked of money. Either Wells had married rich, or he had other sources of income besides a U.S. government pension.

Al-Hassan, maybe?

His thinning dark hair had been styled by a pro. Wells wore a cashmere V-neck sweater and obviously expensive pants. On a hot summer day. But the room *was* freezing.

"This is my partner, Jacqueline Miles," Graham said. "We'd like to ask you a few questions."

Graham hadn't said five words to Jackie herself during their entire drive to Chevy Chase. After her failure to meet Casey at the institute yesterday, he was still seething. Graham would confront her about that, but they had business to conduct first.

Wells smiled, his eyes a steely gray.

"Still in the spy game, Warren? Or whatever you call yourself now?"

Graham felt Jackie tense beside him. He guessed she didn't want to be here. Or was she waiting for Graham to blow up? He waved her to an armchair then took a seat on a sofa. He noted that Wells sat across from him with his back to the wall, able to see out the front windows. So did Graham. Wells must have seen them approach almost before Graham turned into the drive.

"We're working on a case. Obviously, I can't tell you much about it." *Or the fact that it's connected . to my ex-wife.* Instead, he filled Wells in on yesterday's homicide.

"Yeah, I saw the murder on the news last night. You were there?" When Graham didn't answer that, either, Wells said, "Still keeping the low profile?"

Graham wanted to wipe the grin off his face.

"The victim lived with a guy whose name seems familiar. Does Brian Dunlap mean anything?"

David Wells pondered the question. "Can't say it does. He did the job?"

"We're looking for him. We'd like to talk to him."

Wells's tone hardened. "And you think I can help?"

The scant background session was over. Graham leaned forward, resting both forearms on his thighs. He drilled Wells with a look.

"I think he's connected to the team."

"The original twelve?" Wells smiled again. It didn't light his eyes this time, either. "That's a stretch. I assume the name is an alias." Then the impact must have dawned on him. "You mean one of us has committed another human rights violation?"

Graham shot a look at Jackie. Her eyebrows went up at the task force, and now C.A.T.'s, euphemism for *murder*.

"Let's say the guy is a suspect. For now." Graham had reached the real reason for his visit. After revealing information about the single gold cuff link found at the murder scene, he said, "You still have your pair, too, Wells?"

The man bristled. As Graham had expected he would. Was the outrage for real, or for show?

"You think *I'm* involved in this? Whatever it is, I know nothing about it. I retired two years ago. I sell insurance, damn it. I don't need this—" He broke off without uttering the curse word and shot to his feet. "You've said what you came to say. Thanks a lot." He glanced at Jackie. "Now take your little spook friend and get out of my house. I can't believe you'd ask me a thing like that!"

Graham rose, too, then sauntered to the door. Jackie stayed right behind him, so close she felt plastered to his back. Graham opened the door for her.

The edginess he'd felt ever since finding Marilee Baxter dead in the garage, and the anger he still carried toward Jackie for stranding Casey yesterday, turned his mouth into a grim, straight line.

When David Wells followed them outside, Graham turned to face him. Behind Wells in the driveway, Graham saw a glistening, low-slung Maserati. Looked brand-new. He let his eyes return to his ex-team member.

"Nice car. Must have set you back plenty."

David Wells couldn't sell enough insurance to pay for such fancy wheels. Graham ushered Jackie to his own Chevy Blazer. He could feel the hairs on the back of his neck prickle. David was watching them. Graham had never liked turning his back on Wells, either. He didn't like it now.

In his mind, David Wells had sold out. To someone.

Or was he simply the type of high-maintenance overconsumer that Graham didn't have much use for?

In either case, he hadn't answered Graham's question.

AT THE HEARTHLINE BUILDING, Graham rode the elevator to the seventeenth floor. Using the momentum of his anger at Wells, he steered Jackie into a huddle room at the end of the hall. Then he shut the door with an ominous click that sounded more like the hammer dropping on a gun. He had waited long enough. Graham turned on the redheaded operative, his temper exploding.

"I don't seem to be making myself clear."

Surprise shot into Jackie's brown eyes.

"I thought I asked you—in plain English, in words of one syllable—to meet Casey at the Guide Dog Institute by five o'clock yesterday. Where were you?"

Jackie's gaze fell.

"You knew where you needed to be, and when," Graham said. "You should have been there."

"I meant to do you the favor, but right before I left here, I was searching the cell phone logs, like you asked me to." She was trying to make it his fault. "I lost track of time. I'm sorry."

"Sorry doesn't cut it. You obviously didn't understand the most important part of my request about Casey."

Jackie blinked but said nothing.

"My wife is blind."

"Ex-wife," she said. "When I looked up, it was already four-thirty."

Graham took a step toward her. "We may be partners—but don't cross me again."

She shrugged, infuriating him further. She knew his had been a personal request, and he could do little about her refusal to comply. "Maybe you should ask yourself another question." Her cheeks flushed. "How do you still feel about your ex-wife?"

"That's none of your business."

Frankly, he didn't know. Graham tried to suppress a quick wave of desire. That's all it was, he told himself. Just the memory of Casey's green eyes, her dark blond hair, her silky skin, her enticing breasts....

He wasn't about to examine his own emotions.

Sensing the situation deteriorating, Graham threw up his hands. "You know what I'm talking about, Miles. She could have been hurt. Or worse. Without Willy, I'm sure she would have been. And I would have come down on you then like a full-speed locomotive."

Jackie marched to the door, but Graham knew he'd gotten his message across.

She had no sooner disappeared when the door slammed open again and their boss walked in. He'd brushed right past her in the hall. Apparently he didn't need to confront Jackie.

"Where were you and the redhead today?"

"We had an appointment. Someone," Graham improvised, "who wants to sell Hearthline a new software program. We went to check it out. The demonstration—"

Ernest DeLucci blew out a breath.

"And what is your job here?"

"Data analysis," Graham murmured. Not his usual task. "Faster, better, bigger…that program could cut our time in half."

DeLucci scowled, the expression drawing his dark beetled brows together. "Speaking of time, your report on a recent threat assessment in Dubai was due on my desk by noon. You skipped out of here yesterday, then again today. What's going on, Wilcox?"

I wish to hell I knew.

His use of Graham's cover name was a reminder of his mission, and he wouldn't tell DeLucci about his visit to David Wells. Or about the lone cuff link. He stared at his thick-set supervisor for a long moment, taking in DeLucci's dark suit and dark hair. But if the man had terrorized Casey in that revolving door, Graham would have recognized him. Which didn't mean he couldn't be involved in some way.

"Sorry. I'll have the report to you within the hour."

"See that you do." Displaying the perfect round of bare scalp at the crown of his head, DeLucci stalked back into the hall. He spoke over his shoulder. "I am getting sick and tired of the feet-dragging around here. This agency has a critical job to do."

And so do I.

"It'll get done, sir."

He didn't imagine that telling DeLucci the two were intertwined would be advisable. DeLucci was a functionary. Only the director of Hearthline Security knew that Graham and Jackie had been embedded here.

It was better that way, too.

DeLucci was already on Graham's list of possible leaks to Al-Hassan. Like Jackie's favorite, Eddie Lawton. Now Wells had joined them.

Never rains, he thought, but it pours.

Graham ran a hand over the back of his neck. His muscles felt tight, coiled like bedsprings. He needed a break. Needed to reassure himself that Casey was coping with yesterday's murder. Needed to erase the haunted look in her blank eyes.

Which made him think of Rafe Valera.

As soon as Graham filed his report with DeLucci, he'd be on his way to her apartment—for more reasons than one.

Valera, too, was on his list.

GRAHAM LET THE DOOR to the huddle room slam behind him. He strode down the hall to his own office, the one next to Jackie's, and sent that door crashing shut as well in its frame. That didn't help, either.

He started to march toward his desk to complete the overdue threat analysis report, only to find a skinny figure in khaki pants and a rumpled T-shirt hunched over his computer. His chair was already occupied.

Graham spun it around.

Eddie Lawton's bleary eyes blinked at him from behind owlish, dark-framed glasses. Graham withered him with a look.

"Why are you in here?"

His too-mild tone told the computer techie he was a breath away from throttling him just for the hell of it. DeLucci was still on his mind. So were Jackie and Valera.

Eddie's long, spiny fingers stayed on the computer keys. "The usual," he said. "Trying to unsnarl a problem with our server. In the process, I thought I'd update your operating system."

"I did not request your services."

Eddie shrugged. "It's a departmental thing. The server, I mean. The whole network in this part of the building has been down half the day." Eddie scraped back his unruly brown cowlick. He blinked at Graham, all innocence. "You don't believe me, dude?"

Graham ignored the term. He didn't need to be pals with Eddie Lawton. "Whether I do or not isn't the issue."

Eddie shook his head. "Now see, that's working here at Hearthline for you. Everyone's twitchy."

Graham fought the urge to grab him by his shirt. Lawton gave him the creeps. He had the feeling that Eddie was slithering around the building much of the time, especially in the data analysis section, poking into things. Maybe Jackie was right about him.

"Listen, you. I deal with classified information. Nobody," he said, "and that means you, Lawton, *nobody* enters my office without permission or an invitation. I didn't send you one."

"Uh-oh." Trying on a bland smile that didn't reach his eyes, Eddie scooted off the chair. "I'll just be on my way, then. Fix somebody else's glitch who's way more friendly." He slid past Graham to the door and wrenched it open. "If you need help, next time call 911."

"SURE, I'LL HELP YOU," Rafe said.

In desperation, Casey had dialed Anton's number.

She couldn't get Marilee Baxter off her mind.

Even without her vision, she harbored a vivid picture of the previous day's scene in the garage. The cops all around. The smell of evil in the air. Perhaps that was even worse than the reality. Because she couldn't see, Casey painted gory mental swathes and streamers of red everywhere.

Blood. Violence. Death.

She hadn't slept last night. She couldn't eat.

She needed activity.

Yesterday's lesson at the institute had given her some handy tips for working with Willy and coping with her disability, plus a brief measure of control. Or so she'd thought until she'd felt that man behind her on the escalator in the Metro. Did he own a pair of gold cuff links? she wondered.

It was Rafe, not Anton, who had answered the phone.

"Pop's not home. He's at the dentist and I just got in. No problem," he said. "I can carry your laundry and help get it started. I'll be right over."

Casey felt a faint twinge of guilt. Graham had "advised" her not to leave her apartment building.

So she wouldn't. The laundry room was only one floor down.

Despite Graham's suspicions, she didn't fear Rafe, and he was clearly an able-bodied man. Tall, wide-shouldered, broad in the chest, heavily muscled. Casey wondered, as she had more than once, why Rafe wasn't at his job. Assuming he had one, which made her wonder, too, why he owned a .357 Magnum. But if she needed protection, he was it.

Minutes later, Casey had the washer started.

"This isn't so hard," she told Rafe with a big smile.

"I carry the basket, Willy totes the box of dryer sheets in his teeth, you bring the detergent."

"And rinse out the measuring cup." She carried it

to the small counter at the sink. With the fingers of her left hand, she marked the distance from the edge then set down the cup, nudged against the tip of her hand. "I got an A in occupational therapy yesterday."

"You did good, Casey."

When his big hand settled on her shoulder, she started.

"Sorry," he said. "I should have warned you. Guess I could use some training myself. You're doing fine. That's all I meant to say." He hesitated and she imagined the concerned look in his dark gray eyes. "But I sure wish I knew who was responsible for that hit-and-run. Not to mention yesterday in the Metro. Or that jerk with the revolving door."

His tone assured her that he felt as angry as Graham about her "accidents." She leaned close for a hug to show Rafe she trusted him—even when Graham didn't—and felt the hard press of steel against the side of her breast. He was wearing his gun.

Casey jumped back. Talk about protection. Or was Graham right? Did he mean her harm? When Willy nudged her leg, she seized on the excuse.

"Darn. He needs to go out," she said, edging toward the laundry room door.

"I'll take him." Rafe didn't mention the gun. So neither did Casey. "Don't worry," he added. "We won't be long. I'll be watching the front door of the building the whole time we're outside and the lobby is locked. Stay right here and I'll come get you."

"That sounds like a plan."

But when he and Willy left the laundry room, Casey leaned against the dryer and listened to the washing machine clank. Her heartbeat racing, she remembered the gun. Was she locked inside with a killer, rather than keeping the killer out? In the warm, damp space she gave herself a pep talk.

She was fine, Rafe had said.

No problem.

She needed to trust him. Trust her instincts.

He'd be back in a minute. He and Willy.

They were guarding the door. Guarding her.

She was safe. With him.

Still, Casey remembered yesterday when she'd waited and waited for Jackie Miles. If Rafe didn't come back—

"Here we are. Willy's a good dog," he said, his deep, firm voice sending the blood rushing from her head to her feet. Casey sagged against the dryer.

Safe.

"You didn't have to hurry," she said.

She was unloading the washer when Rafe's cell phone rang.

"It's my dad," he told her, checking the caller ID. After a brief conversation with Anton, Rafe hung up. "Wouldn't you know? I just get back and he's outside. Forgot his key. He forgets so much these days," Rafe said sadly. "I need to go let him in. You and Willy come with me this time."

Had he seen her clear-as-glass anxiety?

Casey stayed in the building's small lobby while Rafe opened the main door. Willy panted lightly beside her. He was rapidly becoming Casey's security blanket. She listened to Rafe cross the lobby…heard him open the door. Heard Anton's grumble about him taking too long. Heard Rafe apologize, then offer to carry his father's packages from the cab outside. Apparently, he'd gone to the grocery store after his dentist appointment.

Then, while they were arguing with affectionate good humor out on the sidewalk, she heard someone else's shoes make barely a sound on the tile floor. Inside.

Before Casey knew it, she had been shoved into the elevator.

Without Willy.

In the next second the clunky mechanism engaged, and she was rising from the ground level.

Casey's pulse tripped, hard. She was alone in the car.

No other sounds, no smells.

Just the memory of a hard hand pushing her inside—like into a revolving door.

Casey fumbled for the buttons on the wall panel. The small bumps beside the numbers meant nothing. She didn't know Braille. If she pushed one button, or the whole bunch, she wouldn't know which floor she was choosing. Where she might step out. Who might be waiting for her.

In the lobby the man could see the floor indicator—just as at Hearthline. He'd know where she was.

Where was Rafe? Anton, and Willy?

Suddenly, the elevator car jerked to a halt. Then there was silence.

Except for Casey's pounding heart.

She was trapped. The doors didn't open.

Where was she?

Between floors? Stuck?

Where had Rafe gone? His father? Willy? She would welcome that gun of Rafe's now.

Oh, God. The darkness, so familiar lately, threatened to smother her. She didn't like small spaces. Escalators. Revolving doors. This elevator.

"Help!" she shouted. "Help me!"

But no one answered. The car didn't move.

Casey threw her head back. And screamed.

Chapter Seven

Graham stepped out of his car in front of Casey's building and heard her scream. The blood-curdling cry streaked down his spine.

He ran past a puzzled-looking Anton Valera standing on the sidewalk, vaulted over a mailman's wheeled cart, took the concrete steps to Casey's apartment building three at a time, then stopped dead at the locked lobby door.

He was punching buttons at random on the intercom panel, hoping someone would admit him, when he spied Rafe Valera inside. He wouldn't hear Graham all but soundlessly trying buttons. Valera was staring up at the floor indicator for the elevator as if frozen in place.

"Open up!" Graham pounded on the glass.

Valera noticed him then but took his time getting to the door.

Graham grabbed him. "Where's Casey?"

Rafe's gaze shot to the ceiling above their heads.

"In the elevator. Between floors two and three."

Graham didn't waste time. He'd interrogate Valera later about what Casey was doing in an elevator, alone, with him on the street level. Surely he'd heard her yell, too.

Had *he* rigged the elevator to jam?

Right now Graham didn't care. Casey would be terrified. Blind and helpless, how would she cope with this latest "accident"?

After submitting his report to DeLucci, Graham had left Hearthline to check on her, and in fact to tell her about a new development.

Knowing he shouldn't trust Valera, Graham took a chance and turned his back. First, he had to free Casey.

He headed for the emergency stairs. Within seconds, he stood in the third floor hallway. The elevator car was stuck, all right. And Graham shook his head in disgust.

Someone had crudely wedged a two-by-four into the doors, preventing the elevator from rising the rest of the way to the third floor. Casey's floor.

Behind him, the emergency door opened again and Rafe appeared, not even breathing hard. Graham set his jaw and then his shoulders.

"Help me pry this thing out of here."

To his credit—this time—Rafe didn't hesitate.

Together, he and Graham dislodged the stout piece of lumber. Then Graham jabbed the button that would bring the car up.

When the doors opened, Casey literally fell into his arms. "Oh, God, thank you. I was so scared."

Graham held her tight. He rested his cheek against the silk of her hair. He breathed in, deeply, of her scent: soft, feminine, clean. No artificial perfume. He smelled a trace of shampoo that hinted of coconut, but mostly he inhaled the aroma of Casey herself, female pheromones and fragrant skin and just…Casey.

For a long moment, he couldn't speak.

The hit-and-run. The revolving door. The subway threat. Marilee Baxter's death. Now this. If he'd ever had doubts about her first "accident," they were history.

Someone wanted Casey dead.

To Graham's surprise, he must also want to terrorize her until she couldn't think or move or breathe without fear flooding through her whole body again.

But, damn it, *why?*

After finding the cuff link, he had his suspicions. After talking to Holt Kincade, he had another reason to suspect Valera. Still holding Casey, Graham turned to Rafe.

"What's your part in all this?"

At the moment Valera seemed to have more presence of mind than Graham. But then, he hadn't just nearly lost his ex-wife to a vicious, sadistic killer. Now a few curious tenants were poking their heads out into the hall.

"Let's get inside."

Rafe steered Graham and Casey to her apartment. Leaving them in the hall, Rafe checked to be sure the area was secure. An act for Graham's benefit or real concern? He noted that Valera knew how to conduct the systematic search. When he motioned an all-clear sign, Graham ushered Casey inside to the sofa. He didn't trust himself to speak yet.

Buying time while Valera ran back downstairs to get his father and settle him at home, Graham brought Casey a glass of wine from the refrigerator where she had always kept a bottle of Pinot Grigio when they were married. The significance wasn't lost on Graham, whose hand buzzed from the brief graze with Casey's fingers when he gave her the glass. Despite the different apartment where she lived now, despite his mood—part fear for her, part anger at Valera or whoever her assailant might be—he realized that Casey still kept Graham's favorite wine on hand.

He'd think about that later.

How do you feel about your ex-wife?

When Rafe walked in, Graham dragged the coffee table close so Casey could set down her glass without fumbling for its surface, then spun around to Valera. He caught the other man gazing at Casey with a look in his dark gray eyes that Graham could only describe as tenderness.

The expression on the muscle-packed Valera's face astonished him. It seemed private and only made

Graham more furious. Never mind that Graham had cradled her near only minutes ago, that she didn't belong to him now. That he had driven her away. That he had to keep lying to her....

"Start explaining," he said.

Rafe told him about his father's arrival with the packages.

"I'd left Casey in the lobby, in plain sight. When I heard her scream, I dropped everything and left Pop standing on the sidewalk. But when I charged back inside, all I saw was the elevator rising. And Casey was gone."

Valera risked another glance at her. Graham saw her faint smile, but before she could open her mouth to say "thank you" again, as he knew she would, Graham stepped between her dark, hulking neighbor and his own ex-wife.

"Why was she out of her apartment in the first place?"

Casey explained her need for clean clothes.

"I'd been in the hospital, then feeling weak after I got home, but I also ran out of under—"

Graham cut her off.

"We could have gotten you new clothes. I thought I told you—"

Her lips thinned with temper. "Not to leave this *building*," she said for him.

"Casey. This isn't the time to split hairs."

"You should have been more specific."

"You knew what I meant," he said, tight-lipped.

"I couldn't stay here!" The edges of her mouth were white. "I couldn't stop thinking about Marilee Baxter."

Exactly as Graham had feared. He returned his attention to Valera. He couldn't say what he had to say in front of Casey. With a tilt of his head, Graham indicated the kitchen. "Let's talk."

"Man to man?" Casey said, sounding irritated from her perch on the sofa.

"Man to man."

Graham didn't care whether she liked the idea or even if she despised him right now. He'd done some digging and come up with dirt on Rafe Valera. His other reason for coming here.

When he finished with the muscle-bound hulk, he would warn her in stronger terms to avoid him.

In the kitchen Graham lowered his voice.

"You make me curious, Valera. First, you show up right after Casey's apartment was broken into by a pro. Today, you support her unwise decision to do laundry, then leave her alone. At the mercy of a killer."

Rafe folded his muscled arms across his burly chest. "I live across the hall. Casey needs someone nearby," he said, as if accusing Graham of neglect. "I was right there."

Graham wondered about that, too. Rafe's proximity seemed more than coincidental. Especially after Graham had run a background check on him.

"You're a strong guy," he agreed, then paused for emphasis. "Jamming that two-by-four into the elevator doors would be easy."

"Are you saying *I* tried to hurt Casey?"

Rafe took a defensive stance. Spread-legged, poised for action. Graham recognized it. It didn't surprise him. Neither had the nifty martial arts maneuver he'd seen Rafe execute after the break-in at Casey's apartment. And his obvious familiarity with the .357 Magnum.

Graham had gained both skills for himself during his initial paramilitary training in Virginia at Camp Peary, otherwise known as The Farm.

"Ever been to Williamsburg?" he asked.

As Graham intended, Valera didn't miss his too-casual tone. They exchanged a long look before Rafe glanced away first.

"I don't know what you're talking about."

Graham decided to let the subject go. For now. Almost.

"I thought you might be a history buff—you know, American Revolution and all that?"

He and Casey were looking for more than one man. Rafe Valera was ex-military, a former Special Forces operative, Graham had discovered. Which didn't mean for an instant that he couldn't have changed to some other branch of covert activity or even switched sides.

If Valera had been "bought" by Al-Hassan, he

was a dangerous man to contend with, a turncoat, and Casey was in harm's way. Right in her own apartment. That danger, if not Valera's role, had just been proved.

Giving Graham a look of utter disgust, Valera pushed past him, deliberately making Graham aware of the muscles that roped his hard body, of the brief press of steel sheltered by his shoulder holster.

Graham let that go, too.

Right now he had bigger fish to fry.

In the living room he stopped Valera.

"One more question. What was your fingerprint doing on Casey's answering machine? The police lifted a partial, smeared, but as it turns out, clear enough for a match. Your name just came up in the database."

Rafe didn't look surprised. "Sure it did. My prints are on file from my military service, and I was here with Pop for dinner the night before someone broke into Casey's apartment. She asked me to play her messages then. One of them," he reminded Graham, "about her doctor's appointment the next day. So why would I break in? I already knew where she was going."

Graham saw Casey set down her wine. From the sofa, she tilted her head in their direction.

"What he says is true, Graham. Have you forgotten? Rafe helped free me from the elevator a few minutes ago. You were there, too. How can you persist in thinking he's part of some plan to kill me?"

"I didn't hire him as your bodyguard. He seems to turn up at exactly the right moment to rouse my suspicions."

"He's a friend," Casey insisted. "*My* friend."

Graham's mouth tightened. Her slight frown didn't reassure him. He wondered if she was that certain of Rafe's innocence herself. What had happened in the laundry room?

"Consider this. Valera could have isolated you in the elevator to frighten you. And, in saving you, draw you closer to him."

Her tone was dry. "The one man I shouldn't trust?"

Casey liked Valera, and he certainly liked her, or for his own purposes pretended to. She lived alone now. Without protection. Blind. An easy target.

"I didn't hire you, either," she murmured.

Yet she needed him. "I guess I'll just have to save you from yourself."

Valera started for the door.

"I hate third-party conversations. I'll leave you two to duke it out," Valera said.

Graham followed him. Had he moved into Casey's building in the first place simply to care for his aging father? Or to keep a close eye on Casey for someone else?

Graham had spent enough of his life working undercover to suspect exactly such a move. It was always good to get an agent or asset on the inside, no matter which side you worked for.

He stalked Valera to the door, then let him hear the sharp slide of the deadbolt behind him when he left. Graham waited to make sure he went across the hall. He was putting on the chain, locking himself inside the apartment with Casey, locking out danger, when he heard her cry out again, this time in anguish:

"Graham, where is Willy?"

WILLY WAS NOWHERE to be found.

Until now, in the chaos of Casey getting trapped in the elevator, the dog hadn't been missed.

"I never saw Willy once I left him with you in the lobby," Rafe insisted.

Casey's first thought had been to ask him, but she soon regretted that. Although he had probably been the last person to see Willy, he and Graham had words again, this time about the missing guide dog. Their voices from the kitchen earlier had been muted by their obvious determination not to let Casey hear their lowered voices, but she guessed they had argued then, too, before carrying their quarrel into the living room.

Anton didn't know where the dog had gone, either.

"He helped me, Casey, by holding one of my grocery bags," the older man said, sounding distressed.

"That was the other day, Pop," Rafe said gently.

Anton thought for a moment but only came up with, "It was the deli cheese and meat…but then, he came out the side door, you know, where the super lives, and went with that nice man who stopped to chat with us. He said he'd take Willy to the park for a walk…."

"What man, Anton?" Graham's voice had tensed.

"A man wearing a dark suit. He loves dogs, he said." Anton's voice became fretful. "He promised to take good care of him. I'm sorry, Casey. Was that wrong? Is it my fault he didn't come home?"

"Of course not," she assured him.

There was nothing to be gained in blaming Anton. Dismayed herself, Casey walked every inch of the nearby pocket park with Graham, who asked questions of every other dog owner they met.

No one had seen Willy.

By the time she and Graham returned to her apartment, it was nightfall and Casey was trembling, not merely from the cooler atmosphere in her living room. If a sighted woman like Marilee Baxter had been murdered, what chance did Casey have?

Without Willy—

His absence, a potential dognapping, made her angry, which Casey preferred to feeling helpless. She moved close to Graham on the sofa, felt the welcome heat of his body.

"We have to find him, Graham."

"We will." But he didn't sound confident. "I've called the SPCA. They'll keep a look out for him, call us if someone brings him in. I gave Holt Kincade a ring, too. The D.C. police will watch, as well. Tomorrow—if Willy doesn't turn up before then— we'll hang posters all over the neighborhood. I'll make them on my computer tonight. I already posted a Lost Dog notice here in your building lobby and the laundry room. And we'll put an ad in the papers."

Casey subsided against him, relishing his solid feel. "There's nothing else we can do."

Graham slowly stroked her arm, warming her clear through. He tried to cheer her. "Dogs are good navigators. You've heard those stories in which they find their way home, sometimes over thousands of miles, even after months of being lost...."

He trailed off. Had her crestfallen face given her away? Casey twisted her fingers together in her lap.

"It's hard to believe he'll just show up at the door. Willy has only lived here for a few days."

"But he's bonded with you in that short time. He even likes me." Graham took Casey's hands in his, and she felt his heat mingled with that ever-present, slow wash of need through her body. "Let's not give up yet."

When he stood up, Graham didn't release her hands. He gently tugged Casey to her feet.

"Want to take a ride?"

"To look again for Willy?" In the car they could widen their search for her missing companion.

"Yes. But I also don't want you to stay here tonight alone. Let me pack a few things for you. Then we'll drive over to Georgetown."

Casey's pulse thumped. The beautiful, trendy neighborhood wasn't far away. From her apartment near Dupont Circle to Graham's home just off M Street would take only a few minutes. Yet to Casey, it would seem like a lifetime. Another world, in which she could see. In which he still loved her.

Shaken after Willy's mysterious disappearance and her latest mishap in the elevator, Casey felt tempted to escape the scene of yet another threat to her safety. But she wasn't sure she could handle that particular route.

"I'd rather not," she said. "Anton's right across the hall—"

"No good. I think he has serious health issues."

"—and Rafe is there. I know you don't get along—"

"I refuse to let you rely on Valera." With that, Graham left her standing by the sofa. Casey heard him breeze into her bedroom and begin opening drawers. End of discussion.

Then a knock at her front door changed her view.

In a heartbeat, Graham was in the room again, as if in a race with Casey to answer.

She heard Rafe's low, deep voice from the hall.

"I've been cleaning out Pop's stuff," he said past Graham to Casey. "I came across something that belongs to you." He pushed into the room, ignoring Graham, placing a small carton in Casey's arms.

From its shape and weight, she knew what it was.

So did Graham. "This box has been missing since Casey was hurt. When she left the hospital, she didn't have it."

His accusing tone didn't fluster Rafe.

"You know how forgetful Pop can be," he told her. "He says now that he brought the box here one night after visiting hours. Said he thought you'd have too much to deal with when you came home." Rafe paused. His voice turned sheepish. "Flowers, gifts, all that."

She hadn't received many flowers. Didn't know people here, except for Rafe and Anton, Graham and Jackie Miles.

"That was sweet of him," she said.

"Yeah, well, he then proceeded not to remember where he'd put it. The box has been in the back of a closet ever since. I hope you didn't need what's in there."

"Just a few memories." Not even hers. Casey set the carton on a table. "Thank you, Rafe."

"Pop's real upset," he added. "Worried that you'll be angry with him because he forgot. And after Willy disappeared—"

"Please tell Anton I could never be angry with him. He's my very favorite person."

Rafe's voice thickened. "That's nice, Casey." She

heard him draw himself up, then move past Graham again, who had remained silent and, as usual, disapproving of her neighbor. "I'll tell him. Have a good night."

Casey doubted that.

When Rafe left, Graham finished packing for her. He dumped the contents of the box into his duffel bag, and within minutes they were on their way to Georgetown.

Without Willy.

Casey struggled against her growing sense of loss. According to Graham, she was not to depend upon Anton or his son. She couldn't rely on Willy now either. That left only Graham.

And a trip she dreaded, back into her own memory.

Into heartache.

Their marriage.

Their house.

For the first time since yesterday in that garage smelling of murder, Casey wondered if her own assailant wasn't preferable to spending the night with her ex-husband.

And her own undying need—not only of his protection—but of *Graham.*

Chapter Eight

"This was a mistake," she murmured. "Please, Graham. Take me to a hotel." *Then leave,* but she didn't say that. "I'll be fine there. No one will know where I am."

But for once in his life, Graham observed the speed limit. Casey didn't want to visit their former home and he couldn't blame her. The closer they came to his address, the slower Graham went.

Maybe he wasn't ready, either, to face what had happened to them, to their marriage and all those plans for a future together.

At his corner, he slowed for the right-hand turn off M Street. "Typical summer evening in George-town," he told her like a tour guide. "The narrow streets are jammed with people out to have a good time, eating, drinking, talking, laughing." Graham waited for a couple to stroll across the intersection. "Two people at ten, no eleven o'clock," he said, using time as a means to orient her, "heading down the next block of crowded restaurants and bars and shops still open for business."

He waited some more until an impatient driver behind him laid on the horn of his Lexus. In the passenger seat of Graham's Blazer, Casey started. And, checking the car behind him, Graham silently cursed.

"Some guy with bad manners," he said.

She was already suffering from a case of shredded nerves. Now because of his own reluctance to get home, he'd only made that worse.

"You'll be safer at the house," he insisted.

But would he?

Would *they?*

Graham swung onto the tiny uphill street then gently touched Casey's hand. She had her soft lower lip caught between her teeth, and despite her obvious distress, Graham bit back a groan as heat flashed through his body.

He remembered that mouth.

He remembered everything.

Apparently, so did she.

Graham stalled some more. To make sure they weren't being followed, which was entirely possible, he drove past the black-shuttered, cream-painted brick town house he had shared with Casey. By the time he felt satisfied they weren't being tracked, he'd driven a circuitous route from Georgetown to Dupont Circle and back again. Graham hit the remote control on his garage door opener and whipped inside the darkened space.

"It's okay, babe." He pried her tense hands apart, but the familiar flash of need when they touched only made her jerk away. "We'll be all right here."

Her silence spoke volumes.

She didn't believe him.

When Graham unlocked the back door and ushered her into the kitchen—a kitchen she had planned and decorated—she was shaking again.

Damn.

"A before-dinner drink?" he asked.

"No, thanks." She stood on the threshold of the room, as if remembering its red-and-white decor, the big gas range she'd chosen, the polished wooden floor, the etched glass shutters at the window over the sink, the hanging asparagus fern she'd nurtured there. Guiltily, Graham realized he'd forgotten to water it. Again.

Casey couldn't see the damage.

But that didn't soothe him, either.

She could probably sense it. Smell it. Even hear it.

"Hungry?" he asked, getting desperate.

"No. I lost my appetite in that elevator."

All right. They'd talk about the threats to her then. Safer topic, he thought. The investigation was on both their minds, anyway.

"Case, I think you should know, Rafe Valera was

trained as a Special Forces operative. He knows his way around that gun. He knows how to kill."

Her gaze widened. "Rafe would never hurt me."

Graham's voice tightened. "How do you know?"

"I just do." She shrugged, as if embarrassed. Her cheeks were pink. "He doesn't, uh, give off that aura of menace. Not the same at all as the man who broke into my apartment or threatened me in the subway."

Graham frowned. "Those were two different men."

"They both send out the same signals. Rafe doesn't."

Graham disagreed. "He could be a master of disguise. He could be a damn liar."

"He didn't try to lie about that fingerprint. He owned right up to it." Casey half smiled. "I think the issue's simpler than that. I think you're jealous of him—and our friendship."

Graham's heartbeat kicked up. She knew him too well.

Remembering his quarrel with Valera, he forced a lazy smile, even though she couldn't see it. It had been a while since Casey tried to tease him.

"I wouldn't let the green-eyed monster, or even your obvious affection for Valera, distract me from the truth. For instance, what does this guy do for a living now?"

Casey's smile faded. "I don't know. He never talks about it. Whatever he does, Rafe is gone for chunks of time, sometimes days. And I watch over Anton—or I used to." She frowned. "Then Rafe is home, for equally long periods. I've wondered about that myself. Maybe he's a fireman," she suggested.

"Yeah, right. Whether you like it or not, babe, I'm going to keep digging. Sooner or later I'll find out who he really is and whether he means you harm. In the meantime—"

"Find out how?"

The question stopped Graham cold. Hearthline's data banks, the Pentagon and FBI didn't seem the wise answer. Even if they were true.

Hating himself for the half lie that would substitute, Graham ran a hand over his neck. He was no better than Valera.

"Holt Kincade. Washington PD."

Casey's expression told him she didn't quite buy that, but Graham wasn't about to elaborate. He steered her to a chair then, and overlooking her refusal of food, set about building a couple of Dagwood-style sandwiches from the deli contents of his fridge. Graham rarely cooked for himself these days. Casey's state-of-the-art stove hadn't seen a drip of grease in weeks. But Casey wouldn't let the subject go.

"How do you know Detective Kincade?"

Graham hesitated. "Old buddy from the squash courts at the fitness center we belonged to when you and I first moved to D.C. Holt and I don't play much anymore."

"But he just happens to be assigned to Marilee Baxter's murder case. Which happens to relate somehow to the person who is trying to kill me, too," she said. "And to your old team."

Her obvious skepticism sent Graham's pulse into overdrive. Not to mention the security leak at Hearthline.

"Casey, it happens. Fortunately for us," he added. "My acquaintance with Kincade may get us a closer look at the facts than we'd otherwise deserve." He set the sandwich in front of her. "Now let's eat." He dragged out a chair across from her. "Your ham and cheese is at two o'clock on the plate. Pickle at six. Pile of potato chips at nine." He pushed a glass of merlot toward her. "Your wine's at twelve, straight up. Be careful. It's the Waterford crystal my parents gave us."

They ate in silence.

Casey didn't spill a thing. Or break a glass.

She was beginning to cope with her disability, he saw, and though she'd claimed not to be hungry, she concentrated fiercely on their impromptu meal. Graham ate a few bites, then pushed away his plate.

He leaned back in his chair and studied her, masochist that he was. His response was immediate. He felt the familiar thud of desire in every one of his pulse points, and—no surprise there, either—much lower down. Graham shifted in his seat to ease the throbbing discomfort.

Damn, but she was a gorgeous woman. His woman, once. Her recent blindness had dimmed her sight but not her beauty. She was a knockout.

And maybe she was right. He should have taken her anywhere but to this house. Their house.

Because for damn sure, he didn't know how he was going to make it through the night with Casey sleeping here, leaving her unique scent on the flowered sheets she'd bought herself.

As if she'd read his thoughts, Casey glanced up.

"The house smells good. Clean."

"I hired a maid service." Shoot. That sounded bad. "You, um, always kept the place so nice. I knew I never would. Without help." Which only sounded worse.

She tried to smile but failed.

"It's hard to be here, Graham."

"Yeah." He sighed. "I know. But it's the safest place in Washington tonight." He folded his arms. "I'm sorry you can't stand to be in this house again. Or more accurately, to be here with me again."

Casey shook her head. "It's not you." She waved a frustrated hand. "It's me. I've been run out of my own apartment, but I can't keep hiding and not know when this will end. It's bad enough being blind. But then we found Marilee Baxter yesterday—" her voice broke "—and today someone pushed me into that elevator, then Willy—oh God, *where is he?*"

Graham was out of his chair in the next beat of

his heavy, traitorous pulse. Squatting down by her seat, he awkwardly gathered Casey to his chest. He felt the silk of her hair slide over his hands and tunneled them deeper into the thick heat of it at the nape of her neck. He let his fingers massage the tension from between her shoulders.

And felt himself die a little inside.

"Casey. If I could end it now, I would."

Did he mean only the threat to her life that concerned her, Willy's disappearance included—or the stubborn, thick-blooded beat of his heart through every vein and artery, every cell of his body?

His throat closed without being able to say the words.

I can't tell you the truth.

God, he wished he could. What a relief it would be to just *tell her*. Casey could share his suspicions then. She could help him track her assailant. She could curl into his arms tonight and sleep, dreamless and relaxed, her beautiful features smooth again. She could waken in the dark, turn to him...

Another slow roll of desire took away his breath.

He wanted to find her attacker. *Now*. Wanted to take away the threat, forever. For her, he wanted to slay dragons.

He wanted to...

"Ah, Casey."

He didn't finish the thought. *Make love.*

Casey must have sensed it, though. Or read his

husky tone. "Don't." She stiffened her arms, forcing him back. Graham lost his balance. He started to fall but managed to catch himself with one outflung hand to grasp the table. Before he could stand, she was up from her chair and halfway across the kitchen. Running, figuratively speaking. From *him* this time. He was sure of it.

But Casey miscalculated. Her memory of the house and its dimensions, or perhaps the loss of her depth perception, wasn't enough to avoid disaster. When she banged her hip against the end of the counter, Casey cried out. Graham caught her. Despite her protests, he turned her around, his hands running over her body to check for injury. The feel of her sleek skin under his hands sent heat through him. Through her, too?

"Stop." Casey batted him away. "It's just a bruise. I've had worse."

She meant the hit-and-run that had stolen her sight.

The first accident, which he hadn't solved, either.

And now, she was crying. His fault again.

Trying to quell his desire, Graham watched the slow trickle of tears from her eyes, down her pale cheeks, to the corners of her lips. She didn't try to brush them away.

"I can't do this, Graham. I *can't.*"

Did she mean survival? Evading a killer? Or staying with Graham, even for one night? Casey was right. It was crazy. He shouldn't have brought her here. Neutral territory, their former home was not. He should drive her to a hotel, get connecting rooms, lock both doors....

Lock himself away from her.

But first—

Common sense abandoned him. She had lost Willy and she was hurting. But so was Graham. In that elevator he could have lost her again, with everything unresolved between them. How much effort would it take for someone to slide a knife between her delicate ribs, straight into her warm heart? Easier than a hit-and-run, Graham's mind whispered. At the realization, before he considered the foolish thing he was about to do, he pressed her spine up against the same counter she had just struck, had her caged between his arms, had his mouth already on hers.

At their first touch, first kiss, his heart threatened to implode. But it wasn't the first kiss. Ever since that heavenly brush of mouths in his office at Hearthline, he'd been thinking about this. Wanting this.

"It's no good, Case," he murmured against her lips when he came up for air. "You could move to San Diego instead of living at Dupont Circle near all those embassies, you could never set foot in this place again, and we'd still be here. Together."

"That's what I meant, Graham." She twisted her head away from him. "That's what makes this hard."

Graham didn't bother to answer. He didn't let her

go. He was hard all right, beyond reason, and right now he didn't care.

Neither, he discovered, did Casey. To his vast relief, when he nudged her cheek with his, she surrendered. She turned her head again. And with a faint, helpless sound, met his mouth. The soft, full heat of her could have brought him to his knees. Begging.

Instead, Graham pushed closer. He held her to the counter's edge, let her feel the swift, hard rise of his arousal, ground his hips into her firm sweet belly.

When Casey's mouth opened under his, Graham slid his tongue inside. At the smooth, slick contact, the heat in his loins blazed hotter.

"Babe…" He had his hands on the buttons of her blouse, the first one slipping through the hole, when Graham stopped himself.

What was he doing? He dropped his head to hers, their foreheads pressed together. They were both breathing hard and fast, as if they were on a mission, tense and life-threatening at every turn, yet more than partners.

Taking a deep gulp of air, Graham eased back. He touched Casey's face, as if he were memorizing it in Braille, then let his hands slide from her shoulders along her slender arms to her hands. He caught them in his. His voice was hoarse.

"I'm sorry. I shouldn't have let that happen."

Casey still looked dazed. Graham imagined he

did, too. Had their kisses shaken her as much as they did him?

"I told you," she said. "It's the memories here. We shouldn't have come."

"We had to." He stepped back. "You need rest. I promise to behave myself. You want to use our—the master bedroom, or—?"

She shook her head. "I'll take the guest room."

Graham didn't dare guide her up the stairs, didn't dare track her progress, or imagine his own touch at the small of her back. He stood in the entry hall of the narrow brick town house, and watched her climb the steps. Alone.

He called up the stairs. "Sheets are clean. Towels are still in the linen closet to your right."

"I'll find them."

Graham was sure she would. Just as he felt sure he wouldn't sleep tonight.

Instead, as planned, he would make posters on the computer about the missing Willy. Go through his box of "stuff" that Valera had returned. Watch the street. And stand guard.

He had lied again. Casey was in danger, even here. Not only from him.

Graham watched a dark sedan roll past the house.

Never mind the tangle of feelings inside him. Or his own regrets. He couldn't indulge his needs again.

Casey wasn't his now.

And, Graham reminded himself, he had a job to do.

CASEY KNEW she was in even deeper danger now. The very real danger of falling in love with Graham all over again.

When he'd kissed her so unexpectedly, he hadn't just taken her by surprise. He'd taken her by storm. The onslaught of his lips and tongue had wounded her. The soft assault of his mouth threatened to consume her.

She wondered if she would survive, but Casey didn't mean a killer.

In the darkened bedroom next to the one she had shared with Graham, she didn't try to sleep. She'd choked down the sandwich only to please him. He'd been trying so hard to make her feel welcome, relaxed, when neither was possible in this house.

As for spending the lonely night here…she couldn't bear the floral scent of the sheets in which she had always buried a lavender sachet, the downy softness of the pillows. Even the familiar traffic sounds that rushed past the front of the house grated on her nerves.

Restless, Casey slipped from bed to open a window. The warm summer night carried a balmy breeze, and she let it blow across her face as she knelt at the screen. She inhaled deeply.

And then stopped breathing at all.

On the street a passing car slowed then rolled to a stop. She heard its engine purring. She could feel the driver staring at the house. Or was she only imagining things? Was it easier to fantasize about possible violence than to think of Graham?

Of losing her heart again?

Casey touched a hand to her lower lip, still swollen from their kisses. Did his mouth tingle, too? Was he lying awake next door, dreaming about something he couldn't have?

To her relief, the car drew away.

Not knowing what to do about Graham tomorrow, Casey focused on another problem. The worst of her accidents didn't hurt as much as losing the aging golden retriever.

What if Willy went home tonight and she wasn't there?

Would Rafe call about him?

What if this whole thing caused her to risk more than her life—by loving Graham again?

Although they were divorced, nothing had changed. Including her feelings for him.

Casey frowned into the blackness. Or *had* something changed? Her mild-mannered civil servant who pushed papers around a desk at Hearthline seemed to have some strange alliances.

Holt Kincade, for one.

She'd never known Graham to play squash.

What did Graham's police contact mean?

Then there was Hearthline itself. A secretive organization, considering Graham's order never to go there. Exactly what kind of papers did he push?

She'd never been privy to the details of his work, but was it only data analysis? He seemed too familiar himself with Rafe Valera's gun expertise. He'd dealt with Marilee Baxter's murder like a pro.

Casey straightened, then made her way back to bed. Graham's hidden agenda had destroyed their marriage once. She wouldn't allow herself to fall for him again and suffer more heartache. If Graham hadn't called a halt to their kisses in the kitchen, Casey would have, she told herself.

When a car stopped again at the curb outside the house, she tried to stop pondering questions she couldn't answer. And instead listened. The same vehicle? She felt a fresh surge of fear about the car itself but also something more.

What was Graham hiding?

GRAHAM HID BEHIND the draperies in the small study Casey had made for him just off the entry hall. He stared out into the night at the dark sedan idling again on the opposite side of the street.

Clearly, they were being watched.

Damn, if he only had a pair of night-vision glasses, but they weren't standard issue at Hearthline. He could try to get a license plate number anyway, but that meant he'd risk being seen himself.

If only he had his former team members all accounted for....

Graham peered harder at the car across the street.

The driver was obscured by the night. Dark sedan. Dark clothes. Dark features. He'd been careful not to stop under a streetlight.

When the car finally pulled away, Graham breathed a sigh of relief and dropped the edge of the drapery. He stacked the pile of posters he'd made for Willy, ready for morning. But where in hell was Willy now?

Had Casey's assailant—Rafe, or someone else— harmed her dog? Willy's death would be a meaningful sign that she was vulnerable.

Maybe Willy had recognized the man Anton mentioned by his scent. And Willy had been killed, in effect, to shut him up. He had to admit, hurting Casey's dog didn't sound like Rafe, but that didn't let him off the hook, either. He could still be part of this.

Would the man have killed Casey this time, perhaps with Rafe's help, if Graham hadn't shown up in time to prevent her murder?

The image of Marilee Baxter lying dead flashed through Graham's mind again. The blood, the eerie silence, the lone cuff link in her hand.

Since then, Graham had talked to several of his past team members, in addition to David Wells, all retired now and living in suburban Maryland or Virginia. But others were still active and out of the country on assignment, including Tom Dallas, his own partner before Jackie. One of the other men had died in the line of duty in Iraq.

Graham needed to question Holt Kincade next.

His former "squash partner."

The lie to Casey didn't sit well, but then the lies never did.

For those few moments in the kitchen, with their mouths sealed together, their breathing ragged with the need flowing through him like oil through a pipeline, Graham had forgotten about all the danger and uncertainty.

He hoped Casey had forgotten, too.

The heat was still there, and even Casey couldn't deny it, but that didn't mean she intended to take him back. Or that he could allow that to happen. Graham had no illusions about their broken relationship. He wished he could come clean with her at last about his undercover work, but he couldn't compromise his chance to find the security leak at Hearthline—and Casey's attacker—before it was too late.

Never mind his fantasy that she might forgive him. He couldn't admit to his own renewed feelings for her. And expose her to further risk. Maybe after the killer, the *traitor,* was behind bars....

Yet Graham was puzzled.

In those multiple attacks on Casey, why *didn't* her assailant kill her?

He'd had ample opportunity.

More often than not, she'd been alone.

Blind.

Defenseless.

Yet even with other people near, the man couldn't be a complete fool.

The next question in his mind turned Graham's blood colder than that of the dead woman he'd found in the garage.

Was the killer only waiting for the *right* opportunity to strike?

Chapter Nine

In his study with Jackie Miles, Graham closed the door. "Sorry to bring you away from the office," he said, "but I didn't want to leave Casey alone this morning. Or risk returning her to her own apartment."

"I'm just glad you're not really sick."

Graham raised his eyebrows. "I took the day off from Hearthline and stayed home to let her sleep. I doubt Casey surrendered to her nightmares before dawn, any sooner than I did."

To keep himself awake Graham had watched the street for any further sign of the dark sedan, and toured the Internet on his computer.

"I did have some luck. I finally located one former team member, who's now living in Nevada— and claims he owns a full pair of his memorial cuff links. He hasn't been east in several years. He and his wife have one-year-old quadruplets, which keeps them busy." Graham felt a twinge of envy. He and

Casey had planned to have children. "Too busy, I concluded after our pleasant conversation, to buzz into Washington and kill a woman."

Jackie agreed. "The guy seems out of business as far as C.A.T. is concerned. Including treason."

The list was narrowing, yet going nowhere.

And Willy was still missing.

Graham went over the rest of his list of former team members with Jackie. They could be difficult to track. Most of the men still active were deep undercover on assignments both overseas and in the U.S. Still, they kept his mind off Casey, off his desire for her.

Graham did some thinking aloud. "Since 9/11, cooperation among the services has increased. That can be a good thing."

"But the lines get blurred between CIA-sponsored groups and FBI," Jackie put in. "Not to mention any funds provided by agencies we're not even aware of."

"Talk about undercover. Who can say who really puts up the money for C.A.T.?" Graham dragged a hand through his hair. "This new cooperation and interdiction helps, but it can be frustrating, too. I can't even locate people I used to see every day."

"The names have been changed," Jackie murmured, "to protect the innocent."

True. Including his own.

Graham told himself he was getting used to Jackie's dry sense of humor. Maybe he'd even come down on her too hard in the past. If only he could quash his heated awareness of Casey like that.

"So where do you suppose five of these guys might be right now?" he asked.

"Not together, I assume."

Graham frowned. "I have a vague memory of Tom Dallas implying before he left town that another one of the original task force was also going to Kabul. Wish I had a contact number for Tom at least. He'd be a help."

"He could be in a cave somewhere in the mountains."

Graham raised an eyebrow. "More likely he'd recruit an agent for the field to be his eyes and ears there. Someone native to the region. Tom's not dark, so he doesn't look a whole lot like an Afghan. Going after the bad guys himself wouldn't be part of his job description."

Jackie looked over some files Graham had given her, seeming eager to leave.

"Those are my own files you're examining," he cautioned her. "When you ask questions, be discreet."

When she straightened the folders, her fingers shook.

"I'll see what I can find."

"You okay, Miles? You seem edgy."

He was wondering if he was responsible when the words exploded from her, startling Graham.

"This case has me nuts! I hardly know where to go. Everywhere we turn seems to be a dead-end."

He forced a smile. "That's part of the fun. It's why we're here, or rather, at Hearthline."

Which, at the moment, suited Graham. Otherwise, he might give in to his urge to climb the stairs and kiss Casey awake.

Jackie pulled a sheet of paper from her briefcase.

"Well, then. Read. And destroy."

Graham scanned the page of details then let out a low whistle.

"DeLucci really thinks Al-Hassan will strike on Labor Day weekend?" Then time was getting short. "Where'd he get the information?"

"Cell phone. Satellite surveillance. There's been a lot of chatter."

"Or he could have made it up himself. To throw us off track. To cover his own treason."

"How would he know who we really are?"

His pulse thumped. Jackie didn't meet his eyes.

"If he's guilty, he might know. Give us enough rope to hang ourselves."

Graham was already feeding the memo into the shredder by his desk. At the same time he eased the file folders back into a drawer. Jackie looked at them disappearing, her eyes oddly wistful. The files were encrypted, but that might not keep them safe. Jackie seemed to follow his every movement.

"I could hardly tell you about the memo over the

phone," she said. "I was afraid I wouldn't remember all the intelligence. I took the chance with the actual memo."

"That's just it. We can't take chances right now."

Which was why she couldn't keep his files. And why he couldn't fall into bed with Casey.

"Taking chances is part of being on the hush-hush payroll," she murmured, but her gaze still avoided his. When she walked to the study door, Graham noted that her gait looked jerky.

"Let me know what you find on the names I shared with you. I'll work on the rest of that list. With luck, the division of effort will turn up what we need. Fast."

"And if we turn up more than we bargain for?"

Her brown eyes were wide. With fear?

"Another part of the hush-hush assignment," he said.

If Al-Hassan meant to strike soon, they had to learn who the security leak at Hearthline was. Now. Maybe he would set a trap for DeLucci.

"While you're hunting, get me some solid information on that computer geek at the agency."

"Eddie Lawton? I'm not so sure now that he's suspect."

After finding Eddie in his office, Graham had his own opinion. "We need to eliminate or incriminate people."

He didn't walk Jackie out. He swiveled in his

desk chair to watch her hurry from the front door to her car. She looked as if someone were chasing her, and he frowned.

After she drove away, he carried the files across the small room and hid them in the safe secreted behind a blow-up portrait of Casey and Graham on their wedding day.

"HEY, HOLT." Graham slid into the booth at a café around the corner from his house. "I can't stay long. I left Casey at home, but I don't like her to be alone."

"What's up?"

"My question," Graham said after he had ordered his coffee. He'd been itching since earlier that day to talk with Kincade. After his meeting with Jackie, this was his first opportunity. "What else can you give me on Marilee Baxter?"

"You don't watch TV? Read the papers?"

The story had gotten headline coverage.

"Come on. I know you guys don't tell all to the press." C.A.T., so secret it didn't exist, offered nothing.

Holt didn't have to consult his notes. "You already know she was the girlfriend of our boy with the partial license plate and now-missing sedan." He shook his head in apparent frustration. "Other than the garrote that slit her throat so effectively, we have zip. Whoever did her knew his business. The evidence we collected hasn't panned out so far. He left few traces. None useful."

Other than a single cuff link, Graham thought with a twist of conscience. He eyed Holt's badge.

"I take it the all-points hasn't pulled him in."

"Nope," Holt murmured. "Clean getaway."

Graham's pulse sped. "*If* he left D.C."

"You think he's still here?"

He held Holt's blue-green gaze. "Casey had another 'incident' yesterday." He told Holt about the elevator and then Willy. "That's why she's staying with me right now. Her apartment can't provide enough security."

Graham had a full alarm system, motion detectors, a glass-break on the patio sliders. Even that wasn't enough.

"Besides," he added, "her neighbor across the hall bothers me. I don't want her there."

Holt raised a curious eyebrow.

"The name's Rafe Valera. Ex-Special Forces. Handy with weapons. Who knows what he does for a living now, but he takes too much interest in Casey. And he often seems to be around when something happens to her."

"Or he could provide protection."

"Unless he's the one who wants her dead."

Holt had to agree. "If he wants her killed, she wouldn't be able to recognize him."

Because of her blindness. "She might, via some other sense, but she's vulnerable. I won't leave her with him."

Holt looked even more interested. "Sorry I can't shed more light on the murder. Poor woman," Holt said. "I'll let you know if something else turns up, but at the moment a Case Closed doesn't look promising."

Graham shifted in the booth.

"I have a theory."

"Yeah? Based on what?"

"I think our killer, the same guy who wants Casey dead, is an ex-operative."

"You mean like Valera?"

"Him, too, maybe. The big guy is slippery, elusive."

Holt's gaze sharpened. "Meaning C.A.T.?"

Graham's skin prickled. Holt wasn't supposed to know about the group. He couldn't tell him the complete story, even as much as he knew. The Hearthline security leak was the property of the new C.A.T. group, specifically Graham and Jackie Miles, not the Washington police department. He had to walk a fine line with Holt. He also wanted his take.

"More likely," Graham said, "it's some member of our original task force."

"Most of the old group has dispersed." Holt stared into his own coffee cup. "I hear now and then from Chuck Nelson," Holt admitted. "He's selling tractors in Dubuque."

"You believe that?"

"Yeah. I do. He's got a wife and kids, a mortgage.

We must be getting old. Now I'm a servant of the city of Washington."

Are you, Holt? Kincade kept himself in top physical condition. Had he dropped out, like other members of the team, to become a private citizen? A cop? Graham wasn't sure.

"Anyone else you can think of?"

"You," Holt said with an easy smile. "A data analyst at Hearthline. We're all turning into middle-class drones."

Their gazes held. Then Graham sighed.

Obviously, Holt had guessed that Hearthline was only a cover for Graham's real mission. There had been times when every member of that task force had claimed three aliases.

What he said next went against everything Graham knew to be safe, but Holt was part of the old group. He owned a pair of those cuff links, too.

"What if I tell you that a trusted source is in possession of evidence that might crack the Baxter case?"

Holt's blue-green gaze turned wary. "Just the case?"

"That's all I can say. But I have to ask—do you still own a pair of the gold cuff links that were given to the group after Houston?"

"Do *you?*" Holt leaned closer. "What the hell are you asking me that for? What do cuff links have to do with Marilee Baxter's murder?"

"Answer my question."

"Hell, yes. It's not something any of us would toss away or—"

"Lose track of?"

"You mean, during a murder? I knew it," he said in disgust. "Tell your 'trusted source' this. If I find out you removed evidence from that garage, from that woman's body, I'll throw the damn book at you."

"Will you, Holt?" Graham's gaze hardened, too. "I'm not accusing you of anything, but I need to know which member of that twelve-man team is missing one gold cuff link."

"And you think it could be me."

Holt Kincade shot to his feet. He flung down a five-dollar bill for the coffee then threw Graham a nasty look.

"You just lost your inside contact at the Washington PD. You'd better get home. Casey won't be alone for long. I promise you that."

CASEY WAS TRYING to dust the living room mantel when someone pounded on the front door. Graham had a cleaning service, but she'd been keeping busy to distract herself from thoughts of last night. Those breathless moments in Graham's arms still made her heart race.

Then, too, the killer was never far from her mind.

More likely, Graham just had a visitor. The banging continued. Casey tossed down the rag she'd been using and made her way to the door.

How would she know who was there?

Casey didn't have to decide.

Before she reached the entryway, Graham burst in the back door. In short, obviously angry steps, he blew through the house to the door.

Graham slammed it back on its hinges, nearly shattering her eardrums.

"Police harassment?" he demanded of whoever stood on the front porch. "You tell Detective Kincade—"

"We had a complaint. Just checking it out, sir."

"Like hell."

"One of your neighbors claims your dog was barking all night. We ask you to keep it indoors after 10:00 p.m."

Graham uttered an ugly word.

"What is this? You can't get a search warrant this quick so he sends you over here to rattle my chain while the judge finishes his lunch?"

"Graham, what's going on?" Casey asked, alarmed.

"These uniforms are—"

"Just doing our job, ma'am. Your dog—"

"I don't have a dog," Graham snarled.

Casey stepped closer. "I do, Officer. He ran away yesterday. So there couldn't possibly be a complaint."

Graham steered her to the sofa. "Stay put. I'll deal with this."

She protested. "You aren't doing so well."

He left her there anyway and returned to the door. Casey heard a lot of mumbled words and threatening tones, but couldn't make out what they were saying. Graham had stepped outside and shut the door. Just as he'd done with Rafe Valera in her kitchen.

She fumed until Graham came back. He slammed the door hard enough to shake the windows. Casey heard the police car draw away from the curb out front.

"What was that all about?"

"I had to sound out Holt Kincade about that cuff link. He didn't like my attitude. I imagine I'll get served with the warrant within the next couple of hours. He has probable cause," Graham admitted.

"So he's not going to help us anymore?"

"I think I made another enemy." Graham drew her to her feet. When he ran a hand over Casey's hair, his fingers were icy. "It's possible that Holt Kincade is a suspect."

"He could be part of the 'accidents' I've had?"

"One of my team members from Houston has lost a cuff link. When he murdered Marilee Baxter, he left it in her hand. She must have fought like hell for her life, Case." He paused. "Now we're fighting for yours. If the killer knows we have evidence to convict him, he'll stop at nothing to get it back. If it's Holt," he added, "he has the law on his side."

"As part of his own investigation."

Casey knew she wouldn't like what he had to say next.

"We need to leave Washington."

"Graham, I know this has been a crazy few weeks since the hit-and-run, but aren't you being a little paranoid? Rafe Valera, Holt Kincade," she said. "Can't we just stay here?"

"They'll tear this place apart looking for that cuff link, Casey." Graham led her to the stairs. "Pack your things. If you need help, yell. When the cops come back, that cufflink won't be here. Neither will we."

THEY WERE GONE in fifteen minutes.

"I didn't want to confront Holt with the cuff link," Graham admitted. "And I sure as hell didn't actually show it to him. But like Rafe Valera, Holt troubles me."

"Maybe he was just insulted by your query."

"Or he has something to hide."

Graham pulled out of the drive, then headed for M Street and the usual crush of traffic. When his cell phone rang, a quick glance told him Jackie Miles was on the line.

She sounded shaken.

"It's me. I got into some trouble here." She was at Hearthline. "DeLucci found me looking through the cell phone records. Then he saw the list I was working on. But that's not all. I need to see you, now."

"Can't," Graham said curtly, cursing in silence.

"I have something to tell you. It's important."

Her voice quavered, and Graham remembered how agitated she had seemed that morning. "How important?"

"Crucial. I think I know who—"

"Meet me in ten minutes." Graham didn't want to name a place. "Remember where we had coffee that day?"

"Where you chewed me out. How could I forget?"

"Yeah. The same. Be there."

He hung up and turned to Casey.

He looked into her beautiful green eyes then caught her hand. His skin hummed with the memory of the night before and their kisses in the kitchen.

"Holt's out of the picture. I need to see Jackie. It won't take long, but maybe this is better. I can fill her in, then let her handle things here while we're out of town."

"Where are we going?"

The question stopped Graham. He had no idea beyond keeping Casey safe.

"You know any place we could stay? Somewhere remote," he said, "but within driving distance."

He saw the fear on her face. He couldn't help it right now. He would ease her fears, somehow, but later.

"Choosing some bed-and-breakfast in the area won't work. We can't jeopardize other innocent lives in case your assailant tracks us despite my best efforts to evade surveillance."

Graham checked his rearview mirror.

Nothing looked suspicious. But you never could be sure. Taking a serpentine route, he drove to the diner where he'd talked to Jackie before.

Casey had been mulling over their problem. "I think I do know a place." She looked up, not quite pleased with her choice. "My aunt Lila's house has a guest cottage. It's back in the woods but with a clear view of the road and the driveway. She rarely uses it."

"Aunt Lila?" He'd never heard of her.

"She helped to raise me. I lived with her when I was ten years old. When I was eleven, her turn was done and she shipped me off to Vermont, to my uncle's farm."

Graham's heart sank. Then lifted in the next instant. He squeezed her hand before he let it go.

"Bet you never thought all that shuffling around would come in handy some day. Would anyone be likely to connect you to your aunt's address?"

"No. I haven't seen her since I was eleven."

Casey gave him directions.

Since her childhood had not been ideal, Graham wasn't sure the woman would welcome them with open arms. But he would use the devil himself to gain privacy, and time, to close in on a killer.

With Aunt Lila in a separate dwelling, she wouldn't be at risk. Unlike Casey. With him.

He'd also have to deal with another night or more, alone with her and their growing mutual need.

Couldn't be helped. Graham whizzed into a parking space in front of the diner. It looked deserted but the sign on the door said Open. Good.

He wanted to leave Casey in the car, but he would keep her with him. He hoped Jackie had enough sense not to spill top-secret information about terrorism and their undercover stint at Hearthline in front of his ex-wife.

If Jackie misspoke, he'd have to kick her leg under the table. After settling Casey in a corner booth away from the windows, letting his touch linger on her shoulder, he ordered coffee for three. Then checked the entrance for any sign of Jackie.

Come on, come on.

Graham wanted to be on his way before rush hour to Virginia where Casey's aunt lived. The longer they sat here, the more of a chance they took. When he saw Jackie Miles dart from another parking space behind a hulking black SUV across the street, he breathed a sigh of relief.

"Here we go."

The words weren't out of his mouth before the sight of Jackie's stunned white face turned his blood to ice.

Her eyes were wide with panic. At the glass door leading into the diner, her mouth formed a large O of shock. A stricken glance over her shoulder redirected Graham's attention. He looked behind her, and saw a flash of metal in the sun.

A gun barrel!

Graham shoved Casey under the table. Then he was on his feet. Running. Crouching low. Shouting.

"Jackie! Get down!"

She didn't hear him through the window.

A shot rang out.

The bullet exited Jackie's body at heart level and struck the door in front of her with a twang. Blood splattered the shattered glass and blossomed like a rose on her chest.

Graham didn't draw his gun.

He had no clean line of sight. People were passing by the restaurant and on the street. A dark-clad figure was already climbing into the waiting SUV at the opposite curb, then streaking off into the afternoon sun.

He pushed the door, hard.

And Jackie Miles fell, dead, into his arms.

Chapter Ten

Graham checked for any sign of a pulse in her body—there was none—removed her keys from her pocket, then let Jackie slip, lifeless, to the sidewalk.

Sadly, no one could do her any good.

A crowd was gathering, faces shocked, when he darted inside the diner to haul Casey from the booth.

"Come on, babe. Hurry. Let's get out of here."

A siren already wailed in the distance, getting closer. Someone had called the cops. Graham couldn't afford to be detained.

He pushed past the onlookers, hustled Casey into his car and took off down the Georgetown street.

Jackie Miles was dead.

He was on his own now.

He and Casey.

Several police cruisers passed them from the opposite direction. A narrow escape. "If Holt Kincade spots us, I'll be sleeping in a cell tonight," he said.

"Tell me what happened, Graham."

He glanced at Casey, her white knuckles gripping the passenger seat. "I heard the single gunshot." She hadn't mistaken it for a car's backfire.

"Someone killed Jackie."

"Oh, dear God. First, Marilee Baxter...now her."

Casey didn't go on. If she'd asked what connected the two murders, he wouldn't tell her. But maybe she didn't want to know just yet. Like Graham, she seemed to focus on the streets ahead, her beautiful green gaze staring into space. Shattering his own heart.

Just before they reached the beltway around Washington, Graham changed his mind. On a hunch he detoured to the Hearthline building.

"We need to make one stop."

"Is that a good idea?"

"Maybe not. But this could be our last chance. Jackie had nothing on her, but there may be something in her office." Graham parked on the street, avoiding making Casey experience the same parking garage where she'd been run down and blinded.

After five o'clock, the agency would be mostly deserted. He'd have to take Casey with him.

CASEY STUCK CLOSE to Graham in the elevator, breathing in his scent, assuring herself they were still alive. In Jackie's office she took a chair while he rooted through papers on the desk, opened file drawers, threw things into a bag.

"What are you looking for?"

"Anything that will help us find a killer. Damn," he muttered. "I wish Jackie had said something, even over an unsecured phone, before she came to the diner. Someone was obviously watching her, too."

"They seem to be everywhere, Graham."

"Tell me about it." She felt him turn to glance over his shoulder. And stiffen. The air changed behind her, and a man's voice said:

"Working overtime again, Wilcox?"

"Yeah. I—"

"This isn't your office," the man pointed out. "What's so interesting about someone else's desk? Her papers. You know that's all secured before we leave this floor. Where is she? You both missed a committee meeting this afternoon."

It must be Graham's boss, Casey realized from the rapid-fire questions and his air of command.

"I took a sick day. She was doing research at the Library of Congress when she also felt ill. Must be that 'bug' I had earlier. She went home but she had some papers here—nothing classified—that she wants to read tonight. I was feeling better," he added, "and offered to get them."

Casey prayed the lies would suffice. That the police hadn't notified Hearthline yet of Jackie's death.

Graham's employer didn't buy his excuse.

"Leave everything here. Lock it in her file cabinet. She can read tomorrow."

"Or did you plan to read tonight?" Graham murmured.

Ignoring that, his boss paused near Casey's chair. "Who is this? I didn't see any after-hours visitors logged in."

"My wife." The half truth troubled Casey, but Graham offered no further explanation. He didn't supply her name.

The man didn't acknowledge Casey. She could have been a lamp. Nongovernment issue.

"I didn't know you were married," he said.

"This environment doesn't lend itself to idle chatter around the water cooler. Not many people do know."

Graham's tone chilled. "Obviously, she can't see," he said, as Jackie Miles had at the receptionist's desk. "What difference does it make if she's here for a few minutes? The security guard wasn't around when we came in. We're leaving anyway."

"See you in the morning. Be on time."

A drawer slammed. Graham urged Casey toward the door, and she could feel the other man staring after them.

She heard Graham's scowl in his voice. "Damn DeLucci. He never works late. I guess we make do with what we have."

Frowning, her suspicions growing, she wondered why DeLucci had called Graham by another name. *Wilcox.*

HALFWAY TO the elevators, Graham changed his mind. He led Casey back to Jackie's office then retrieved the bag he'd filled with her papers. Lock them up and lose his one chance to find the security leak? Clues to the killer? No way.

Making sure DeLucci had disappeared, he opened Jackie's office door just as the scrawny techno wizard who had been her favorite "suspect" rounded the corner. On worn sneakers, Eddie Lawton screeched to a halt. And frowned.

"Hey, how come you have her keys?"

He had to give the kid points. DeLucci hadn't asked.

His pulse speeding, Graham used the same excuse.

"She wanted me to pick up something for her."

Eddie was shrewder than Graham had thought. "She packed her stuff right after lunch," he said, trying to smooth his brown cowlick. "Told me she was going away for a while."

That surprised Graham.

Eddie peered around Graham through the half-open door. "Her laptop's still here."

Graham seized the opportunity. "That's what I'm after. We're having dinner before she leaves town. I promised to bring her the computer. You worked on it?"

Clearly, Eddie hadn't forgotten his run-in with

Graham. "Yeah," he admitted, seeming reluctant. "Just today. Her operating system—like yours—is outdated. It crashes all the time, but I needed to order the upgrade. Maybe that's why she left it behind." He looked past Graham at her desk. "Did she leave a note?"

Graham shook his head. "It's fine. You know her password?"

"Sure."

Drawing Casey close, Graham checked the hall for any sign of DeLucci. Then studied Eddie Lawton. How well did he know Jackie? Enough to be privy to "crucial" information?

Graham made a decision. If Eddie was part of the conspiracy, he'd clam up. If not, he might be useful. At this point it was an easy choice to make.

"Listen, Eddie. I'm sorry I jumped down your throat before. I need your help. She's in a bit of trouble. I need to look at her computer. Now. She and I are assigned to a project—"

"Yeah. I know."

Before he could go on, Graham took Casey next door to wait in his own office, then hauled Eddie into Jackie's office and shut the door. Eddie stared, as if he'd gone crazy. Again. Graham didn't want Casey to hear the rest.

"What project?" he asked Eddie.

"Finding some security leak at Hearthline. Al-Hassan," he said as if that were obvious.

The statement nearly buckled Graham's knees. "She tell you that?"

Eddie smiled, looking cagey. "Not intentionally. We went out a few times." Maybe that was what had changed Jackie's mind about Eddie as a suspect, Graham thought. "After a couple of beers," the techie said, "she opens up, you know. I didn't ask," he assured Graham. "But bingo, there it was. Right from her mouth. Pretty hot stuff."

Graham scowled.

"Hey, that's all," Eddie insisted. "Just her assignment, the fact that she may not be who she said she was." Eddie paused, while Graham thought, *that's all?* "And that she was working with you. Interesting, huh?"

That's enough. Graham crowded Eddie Lawton against the closed door and eyeballed him for a long moment.

"Listen. Forget whatever you heard. She has some…personality problems," he said. "She tends to embellish a situation, to make herself look, well, maybe more *interesting* to a guy like you. A couple of beers. That's all it was, understand?"

"Yessir."

"Now what's the password?"

GRAHAM AND CASEY were well out of D.C., into Virginia, when he realized they were being followed. The dark SUV stayed with them through several abrupt lane changes. Graham could feel Casey's alarmed gaze upon him.

After Hearthline, he knew she was itching to pound the truth out of him. But she was biding her time.

Graham accelerated and the wind whipped through their hair. He pushed the car, hard. But still, in rush-hour traffic, he couldn't lose their tail.

It looked like the same car from the diner. Was Jackie's killer behind them now? Or were there two look-alike cars, part of a fleet, perhaps, leased by the conspiracy?

"Someone is chasing us," Casey realized.

"Not for long."

Minutes later, he turned off the interstate at an exit onto a two-lane road. It led past the grand old plantations along the James River, which always surprised Graham. Not far from the nation's bustling capital, the hills and valleys of Virginia seemed to be caught in a time warp.

Peaceful. If only they could get to Lila's.

But the other car had followed. It hung just off Graham's rear bumper. He was reaching for Casey's hand to reassure her when a gunshot exploded the rear windshield. The bullet streaked past Graham's head and made a starburst of the windshield in front of Casey.

"Graham!"

Adrenaline pumping, he shoved her head down.

They weren't just being tailed now. What better opportunity would the killer have than to wipe them out on a lonely country road? Then disappear, like Marilee Baxter's killer, and Jackie's. He didn't form the thought before more shots rang out. The next one could take off his head. Or Casey's.

He pulled out his Glock. Taking wild aim, he got off a few shots at the sport utility vehicle behind them before the driver returned more fire.

A blaze of searing heat raced over his skin and Graham jerked in his seat. He felt a sticky wetness begin to trickle down his right arm. He'd been hit.

"Hang on, babe."

She didn't question him now. Casey braced herself. As soon as she did, Graham pushed the car into a one-eighty spin. Time to try out his defensive driving skills from Camp Peary. Slamming on the brakes, he straightened the Blazer then hit the gas again. They sped toward the dark SUV that had been behind them just seconds before. At the last instant, Graham cut away. He could see there was only one guy in the car. Graham didn't recognize him. He would reconstruct his image later. When they were safe.

He spun the Blazer a second time. Casey screamed.

He knew she must be dizzy by now. It couldn't be helped. Better to be a little light-headed than dead.

He knew the feeling. Graham's vision had

blurred, and he felt weak himself. On a short straight-away, he closed the gap between the two cars, putting his Blazer nose-to-tail against the dark SUV. Then, with a solid tap of his left front to its right rear fender, he sent the other car into a spin. Unable to react in time, the driver lost control.

The SUV shot off the road, through a clump of brush, into a ditch, then rammed into a tree. Tilted to one side, it heeled over and the car's wheels spun.

Graham stopped the Blazer. Casey sat frozen, but he didn't try to explain. Gun in hand, he ran across the road and found the driver still alive. His dark features and dark clothes didn't register with Graham, either. It wasn't the guy who had pushed Casey into the revolving door. Shaking his head to clear it, he checked for ID. He didn't find one, which didn't surprise him. The would-be assassin traveled light.

Graham jogged back to the Blazer. He threw it into gear and shot off down the empty road. Casey clutched his arm, making him wince with pain.

"Graham, I need to know what's going on."

He eased away. "Try to relax. We'll be at your Aunt Lila's in a few minutes."

"But that driver—"

"When we're safe, I'll phone the cops. And an ambulance." He glanced at her. "You all right?"

"I'm not hurt." Casey held on, as if she knew he needed to focus on the road.

She was still silent when Graham pulled off the

narrow, winding road and headed down the long driveway between oaks and maples to her aunt's home.

He was sure they weren't being followed now.

But for how long would they be safe?

How much longer could he keep the truth from Casey?

LILA GIBBS had a warm, sweet voice that Casey remembered from many years ago. Since then, they had only exchanged Christmas and birthday cards, but to Casey's surprise, her aunt welcomed her with a huge hug.

"Good heavens, child. Come in, come in."

In the next moment she was standing in Lila's living room, still shaking from her experience on the road with Graham, but taking in the smells and sounds she hadn't known in nineteen years.

The soft tick-tock of the mantel clock.

The rustle of her aunt's starched apron.

The scent of home-baked pie from the kitchen.

The lily-of-the-valley cologne Lila had always worn.

Graham had gone back to the car and Casey wondered how they were going to explain that shattered windshield.

"I was astonished when you called," Lila said in her soft Virginia accent. "Even your voice took me back. I've never forgotten that year you spent with us. Of course your uncle's gone now," she added in a sad tone, "but the rest has stayed pretty much the same."

"I can tell it is," Casey murmured. "I think I can find my way around this house even now."

She could sense Lila's concerned expression.

"You must tell me all about it. But right now, I'll get you settled." She put an arm around Casey's shoulders. "That is one impressive husband you married, by the way. I didn't get a good enough look at him yet, but from what I did see, he looks like a very fine man."

"He is," Casey said, and meant it.

After that highway chase—and the earlier stop at Hearthline—she had her doubts about his honesty. But that was between Graham and Casey.

"Your uncle would approve," Lila said. "He always worried about you. So did I."

Then why did you send me away? Casey wondered. But now didn't seem the time to examine old hurts.

Lila drove with them to the guest cottage at the far side of her property. If Casey had remembered right, the house was tucked in among the trees, and Graham gave it his immediate stamp of approval.

"This will be great." He unloaded their bags then followed Casey and Lila into the cottage. "You have a beautiful place, Mrs. Gibbs."

"Call me Lila. You could stay with me instead," she suggested. "There'd be more room."

But Graham wouldn't hear of it.

"We've had so much upheaval lately, including that deer on the road that nearly came through our windshield, we just want to sleep—and, well, spend some time together." His voice had warmed, sounding of love. "When Casey mentioned your cottage, it sounded ideal."

Casey heard her aunt's soft laugh. "I understand. I was half of a young married couple myself once."

She assumed they meant to make love while they were here, and Casey felt her cheeks heat. She'd just survived the night before in the same house with Graham, and now they were being treated like honeymooners again. Casey could almost indulge the fantasy. Graham was standing too close, his body nearly touching hers, and he slipped an arm around her shoulders. Then he planted a light kiss on her hair, probably to impress Lila.

That slow roll of desire ran through Casey again. Until she realized that Graham's arm against hers felt wet, tacky. The familiar scent of blood reached her nostrils.

He'd been shot!

At the same moment Lila noticed, too.

Sounding shocked, she said, "Graham, you're bleeding."

"The deer," he murmured. "The glass cut me."

"You could have been killed." She hurried off to the cottage bathroom, returning in seconds. "Sit down. I have first-aid supplies," she said for Casey's benefit.

Casey wondered if Lila believed his story about the deer. It was a common accident in the rural area, but he had lied so easily.

Casey couldn't wait to get him alone.

"Aunt Lila, I can clean his cut."

"But dear, your eyes—"

"I have a great sense of touch. I'll have Graham treated and tucked into bed early in no time."

Graham stepped in. "I can hand Casey the supplies and she can be my nurse."

Playing to Lila's impression that they wanted to be alone with each other, Graham shared a laugh with the older woman. As if they'd be playing other games tonight, as well.

Although still feeling that slow burn deep inside, Casey had another agenda in mind.

Lila paused. "I'll leave a basket with dinner on your doorstep. If you don't want to eat right away, you can heat it later in the microwave." To Casey's astonishment, Lila added, "Welcome home, dear," then shut the door behind her.

Her aunt no sooner disappeared when Casey whirled around to Graham. She intended to make sense of all the craziness swirling around them, when Graham suddenly sagged against her.

"I need to sit down."

He was about to pass out. Alarmed, Casey used

her instincts to guide him to a chair. She barked her shin against the kitchen table, but her injury seemed minor compared to Graham's. He'd been struck by a bullet.

"It's just a graze," he insisted.

"That's what they always say."

"Who?" he asked, sounding even more fuzzy.

"Macho heroes in the movies and in books." She pushed back his silky hair. "Put your head down while I sort through these first-aid items for some sterile gauze."

But Graham snagged her wrist.

"Come here. Please."

For a long moment he held her close, resting his head against her front, and all at once Casey was weeping.

"God, Graham. Lila's right. You could have been killed." Like Jackie.

"So could you." He dried her tears. "I tell you, Case, when that windshield exploded—"

"And before, when Jackie was killed...."

"It's been one helluva day. At least we're still alive." He leaned back, as if he shouldn't touch her, and quickly laid out the first-aid kit on the table. "Clean gauze at noon. Peroxide, four o'clock. Try not to hurt me."

Casey bit her lip. "You're a good seeing-eye man." Which only made her think of her missing dog. "But I sure wish Willy was here. My shins take too much of a beating without him. I'm constantly banging into things. Besides," she said with a sniff, "I miss the old guy."

"Yeah. Me, too. Tomorrow we'll call Anton—or Valera. See if they've had any word about him. No one's called my cell phone, which is the number I left on all those posters. And in the newspaper."

For the moment Willy seemed a safer topic than Jackie Miles, the car chase, or the wounded driver. Even mentioning Eddie Lawton, or being dumped in Graham's office while they talked, didn't appeal to Casey right now.

She helped Graham remove his shirt, which heated Casey's blood. With his hand guiding hers to the spot along his bicep, she pressed the gauze soaked in peroxide to his wounded arm. Graham sucked in a breath.

"Damn, that does hurt."

"Sorry. Graham, we should go to a hospital."

"And have them file a report on a gunshot wound?" She felt him shake his head near enough that the slight motion sent another thrill through her body. But when Casey tried to pull back, Graham's other hand pressed her close again.

He smelled so good, of soap and spice and skin. Of Graham. Brusquely, she opened the fresh gauze pad he gave her. His proximity made her want too much. Casey eased away before she surrendered to her worst instincts to wrap her arms around him, to cradle him near, to kiss him again.

"Let's finish this."

For long moments today, she'd wondered whether they would live long enough to reach this cottage, or if Jackie Miles's death would become the precursor to Casey's murder, too.

She dabbed at Graham's arm until he told her the blood had stopped. His hand over hers felt warm, vital, strong, and yet there was a slight tremor in his touch. From loss of blood? From the heady contact with each other? Or, from wanting....

Casey waited for him to cut strips of adhesive tape, then with Graham holding another pad in place, strapped it to his arm. His biceps flexed—from pain, or her touch?

"There. That should do it." As if she might see, she bent her head low to "look" at what she'd done, and her hair slipped over her cheeks, brushing his skin.

Graham inhaled again.

She jerked back, cheeks blazing. Heart thumping. "I'm sorry. Again. I didn't mean to hurt you."

"It hurts anyway," he said. "That's not what I mean."

When his hands came up to cup her face, Casey started shaking again. Not from the day's terrible events, or even running for her life. Now she needed to escape her emotions.

"Don't pull away from me," he murmured.

But Casey did exactly that—even though it took

all her willpower to do so. His husky tone, full of need, lured her to come closer…to give in. To love him.

Instead, she fumbled the tape back into its container.

"Casey."

She might desire him, more than any man for the rest of her life, but she didn't trust him.

In self-defense, she spun back to him and finally spoke the words that had been haunting her all day.

"Who are you, Graham? Who are you, really?"

Chapter Eleven

"Casey, let it go."

"Let what go?" she asked. "Or is it every day that someone chases you all over Virginia shooting out your windshield?" She took a breath. The motion lifted her breasts, but Graham tried not to notice. It should have been easy, considering Casey's anger. "That guy put a hole in your arm, another bullet whistled past your head. And I should just *let it go?*"

Graham's heart beat a slow, thick rhythm. He stood in the center of Lila's cottage and prayed for divine guidance. *Leave it alone. For now.*

"Tell me." She came closer. "What is this about?"

In defense Graham lost his temper. "You know what it's about. The guy in the elevator started this whole thing. Until we find him, we're both in danger."

"I need you to tell me *why.*"

"Because you recognized him. Because—" Graham broke off. *Because my cover is blown.*

If he didn't watch himself, he'd spill everything. And only endanger Casey more. She couldn't know the truth. If she did, and the people who were after them got hold of her, Casey could be tortured for information she was better off not knowing. She could be killed. And even if he was a thousand miles away then, Graham would have pulled the trigger himself.

But she was one step ahead of him.

"He knows you, too."

"I'm not sure, but it looks that way."

Her mouth thinned. "Not good enough, Graham. I lost my eyesight when that car hit me. If you're involved, I think it's time you explained. Everything."

"I can't."

Casey stared at him for a long moment. She was blind, yet she seemed to see right through him. She always had.

Then, abruptly, she turned and walked away, brushing past him. She left her scent behind, and Graham felt his lower body tighten another notch. She stood at the window that overlooked the front yard and the drive. Graham prayed again—that no one was waiting outside in the growing darkness with a high-powered sniper rifle.

He reached out. "Casey, please. Come away from the window."

"Why, Graham? Because I'm a target? I have a right to understand why." She ran her hands over her arms, as if to ward off a chill. Graham felt icy cold himself. The heat in his loins had cooled. He didn't know what to say. "I don't hear your answer," she finally said. "So let me give you my own perspective."

She paced back and forth, still in plain sight of anyone lurking in the shadows. Graham fisted both hands at his sides, but he knew better than to approach her. Casey was angry. She had every right to be.

She was also scared.

Like him.

"Let me see," she began in a musing tone that didn't hide her irritation. "I married a man who seemed to be everything I wanted. A solid, unflappable, steady guy who happened to work for the U.S. government. A guy who handled paperwork, built up a good pension, and came home every night to me— and to the children we would have someday."

"Casey, I wanted that, too. A home, kids—"

"Did you? Really? Then why, instead of staying in one place, did we move all over this country? You worked for this agency, then that one, and six months or a year later, we were off to somewhere else. When we hit New York, I must have been a fool to even try running that gallery. I should have known I'd only have to sell it."

"I can't pick my assignments."

"Obviously, neither could I." Casey's voice trembled. "I grew up in so many different homes, with so many different relatives, that all I wanted was someone who didn't drag me from pillar to post."

He ran a hand through his hair. "I know that's how you grew up. I know you hated that. But we're talking about my job, the one that pays the damn bills."

Graham winced. He knew that was the wrong thing to say the minute he opened his mouth. Macho idiot.

"Yes. I suppose it does. Or did," she added mildly. "But we never gave my career a chance, did we? Just when the gallery was up and running at a profit, when I was making a place for myself in New York, the mecca in my business, what happened, Graham?"

He set his jaw. "Hearthline needed me here." He paused. "And after 9/11, I wanted you out of the city, somewhere safer."

"Washington, D.C.?" She sounded incredulous. "I don't mean to be sarcastic, but it was you and me, wasn't it, who were nearly murdered on the road between there and here? A few hours ago?"

"Right." It was all he could say.

"D.C. was only part of the picture. I see that now. If you weren't 'working late,' you were out of town. Sometimes for weeks. And again, that's the tip of an iceberg." Casey walked the carpet again. "Never mind Rafe Valera. How did you even know what kind of gun he was carrying?"

"I've seen it before."

"Where, on TV? I don't think so. In fact, where

did you get the gun you used today? I've never seen you with a weapon before."

For good reason. He usually kept it in his locker at work, or in a gun safe in his closet, but Casey had never seen either one. He made sure of that.

"And then there's Holt Kincade. Your cop friend. The man I married didn't know any cops unless one was handing him a speeding ticket. He didn't speak their lingo. He didn't steal evidence from a crime scene as blithely as you please. I would have staked my life that he never saw an actual crime, much less a murder."

Graham tried to stop her but she continued.

"What kind of *partner* was poor Jackie Miles anyway? What information did she have for you today?" At the end of the living room Casey whirled around. "And why did your boss at Hearthline call you Wilcox?"

Damn. Graham was so used to his Hearthline persona that he hadn't caught that himself. He crossed the room to her. He grasped her shoulders and looked deep into her eyes. His gaze begged her to understand, to accept, but she couldn't see him, he reminded himself. He couldn't reach her. He had to lie to her again.

"DeLucci's under a lot of pressure from the White House and Hearthline's director. He can be forgetful. Confused. Like Anton, only younger."

Casey ignored that, too. "You once said my hit-

and-run was not only deliberate, but that it could be part of 'a whole hell of a lot more.' I need to know what that means. Now."

She waited while Graham warred with himself. The longer she waited, the more her expression fell. Her obvious disappointment in him made Graham want to open a hole in the floor and crawl inside.

"I'm sorry I'm not what you expected." Desperately, he tried to buy time. "Casey, I wish I could tell you. But I can't. Not now. Not yet," he said.

She didn't need her vision. Her blank, scathing gaze did the job anyway. Casey tore free and stalked past him.

"Then you can go to hell."

CASEY COULDN'T stop moving. Every muscle, every nerve in her body needed action. If she stopped, she might kill Graham herself.

For so obviously lying to her.

For betraying the small kernel of trust she'd rediscovered.

Graham drew the draperies across the windows, then, she assumed from the snap of a switch, turned on the lights. Daring him to stop her, Casey walked to the front door. She was too angry to consider that she might be in danger. She retrieved the box of food Lila had left on the step for their dinner. Had her aunt heard their argument?

Casey wasn't hungry now.

She slammed the door then felt her way across the room. She sensed Graham watching her every move. He'd be feeling helpless, as he always did when they quarreled.

Yet Casey could still hear those gunshots. At the diner. On the road. She could feel Graham's torn flesh beneath her fingers when she'd cleaned his wounds.

Were they really safe here?

Casey remembered the cottage layout, but not well enough. Nineteen years had dulled her memory. In her darkened world now, she carried the box of fragrant-smelling chicken casserole, fresh biscuits and apple pie to the kitchen doorway, inching her way along.

Then she tripped.

With a startled cry, Casey stumbled over the single step that led down to the kitchen. The box went flying. So did Casey. One second she was on her feet, full of righteous indignation. The next, she was lying facedown on the floor.

Graham was beside her almost before she landed.

"I should have warned you about that step. You okay?"

"Just embarrassed. I was so busy showing you that you no longer exist, that I didn't remember the step."

Graham helped her to her feet. The quick graze of their hands, the feel of his strong grip and warm skin sent heat through her before Graham abruptly pulled away. He checked her over, but only with his gaze. Casey could sense it. He didn't dare touch her again.

He picked up the food. Plastic containers had scattered everywhere, apparently. Casey tried to take them from him.

"I can do it, Graham." She held one hand in front of her so she wouldn't run into the refrigerator. With the door open, she put the chicken on the top shelf next to a carton of milk. Or was it really milk? But when she tried to slip the pie plate onto the bottom shelf, something wouldn't budge. The aluminum pie pan started to buckle, and apple juice oozed out over her hands. She licked her fingers.

Coping in a strange place, or even in her own apartment, could be so frustrating. Again, she missed Willy. She missed her darned eyesight.

Graham caught the pie. "Here, let me."

Feeling stubborn, Casey wouldn't let go. Their hands awkwardly overlapping, her skin tingling from his inadvertent touch, they managed to set the pie on the shelf without spilling all its juice.

Still, Casey came away with sticky fingers, and a small smear of apple pie filling had ended up at the corner of her mouth. She must have touched it. When she started to blot the sweet spot, Graham stopped her. He shut the refrigerator door then pushed her up against it.

A bolt of desire shot through Casey faster than that bullet through the windshield. Her pulse hammered.

"Graham, don't." She tried to turn her head away.

"Hold still."

He caught her hands in his, lowered his head, and licked the pie juice from her mouth. His body weight trapped her spine against the cool front of the refrigerator. Then nothing got through to her brain except the feel of his muscles, the hard pads along his chest and the strength of his embrace.

Casey sagged against him. This was how their quarrels had always ended.

When he put his hands on her, she knew she was lost. Angry, yes. Disappointed, sure. But this was Graham. She couldn't seem to avoid him. Or her own feelings.

"Tonight," he said, "we're all alone. Jackie's gone. Holt's gone. I can't go back to Hearthline. You can't go home. We only have each other now."

He had a point but she wouldn't acknowledge that.

"Stick with me, Case. Please. For a little longer. When we figure out this puzzle, then I'll tell you the rest. Right now I can't—"

Casey covered his mouth with her still-tacky fingers.

But Graham licked those, too. She had never known how erotic such a simple gesture could be.

His lower body pressed closer, and she felt the hot length of his arousal through her clothes. Casey's breasts grew heavy, tight.

She whimpered, low in her throat.

"I don't have my vision, Graham, but I can still be useful in stopping whoever's after me—I mean, after us. How can I help?"

"Right now?" His mouth covered hers. "Like this."

GRAHAM'S BREATH shuddered inside him and along the seam of Casey's mouth. When her wet lips parted he slipped his tongue in, deep and slow.

"Ah, babe."

She felt like home. No matter that they were miles from D.C., from his town house or her apartment. After the day they'd shared, how could there be barriers between them? In seconds, he'd gone from anger, sorrow, even fear, to hot and hungry.

He'd never wanted anyone as bad as he wanted Casey. More than his next breath he ached to feel her underneath him, his hardness sheathed again in her slim body as if the whole rotten year of separation and divorce—and these past weeks of anguish and frustration and fear—had never happened.

Marilee Baxter.

The lone cuff link.

Jackie's murder.

Holt Kincade, turning his back on Graham.

DeLucci's latest suspicions. His own. Their flight from Washington, the car chase, the damn flying bullets.

The graze on his arm that stung like crazy and throbbed in every pulse of his body....

None of that mattered now.

Put the danger aside for tonight, he thought. And he tried to impress upon Casey in every kiss, the same need that was flashing through him with every heartbeat.

It pulsed low and insistent, demanding release.

"Casey, I'm sorry. I don't know how to keep you safe without keeping secrets."

She nearly pulled away, but Graham tightened his embrace. He trailed hot kisses over her temple, then along her cheekbone, the edge of her mouth, and down her throat to the neckline of her top. That gentle swell of cleavage seemed to beg for his attention, and Graham nuzzled the first button like an infant seeking sustenance at her breast.

"We need each other," he told her, his voice hoarse on her skin. He lifted both hands to her breasts, cradled them through the thin cotton barrier.

Graham didn't want any more obstacles between him and Casey. Not before morning. Not even then, if he could change her mind about him tonight.

Because right now, her body told a very different story than her words of disappointment in him.

Right now, like the sneaky operative he was, he

would use that need however he could to bond them. Graham slipped her first button free, then hesitated. When Casey didn't stop him, he undid the next one, and the next, her flesh revealed inch by inch until her blouse hung free at her sides. And Graham feasted on the very sight of her.

Too long, he thought. He was starving for her. When he released the clasp of her bra—the plain, serviceable white bra Casey always wore to hide such treasure—he groaned. It turned him on, better than a black lace nightie.

"You're…you are…"

There were no words. Graham lowered his mouth to her breast, first one, then the other. And Casey moaned.

Despite the differences between them, which might surface at dawn, she was still Casey. Sleek, lithe, compact, and just the right fit for his mouth, his arms, his body. She smelled fragrant and sweet, and for a moment he had lost the power of speech. She was clean, innocent, uncomplicated.

Open.

He wanted her to stay that way, not to know about terrorists, conspiracy, impending disasters. That was his job. He hated it at times, like this afternoon on the way to Virginia, and loved it at others when the bad guys lost.

Casey was his retreat, his salvation.

He couldn't tell her that, not yet.

But—for now—she needed him as much as he needed her.

Graham sighed in relief, in appreciation.

Let that be all tonight.

He lifted her, raised her until her breasts were level with his lips, and took his fill.

"Graham…"

With a whimper, she went limp in his arms, her head thrown back against the refrigerator door, her beautiful throat exposed. Graham kissed the throbbing pulse that beat there, the essence of Casey's life. The life he meant to preserve. Then he realized that, although she was aroused, she might also feel uncomfortable.

They needed a bed.

"Wait. Let me check the doors. Turn out the lights."

He knew that didn't matter to Casey. And it made him feel a little guilty. By necessity, he kept things from her. C.A.T. and its shadowy sponsors didn't encourage members to fall in love, marry, have kids. When they did, as human beings will, it wasn't talked about. Some wives knew, some didn't. Casey had been of the latter group, by his choice, and at times his own remorse overwhelmed him.

He took his time securing the cottage for the night. Taking one last look at the dark yard, the driveway, the cover of trees, he saw nothing. Heard nothing.

Maybe they *were* safe. For now.

When he turned from the front door, Casey was standing in the middle of the living room, her gaze not quite on him, her body tense.

It was up to Graham to reassure her.

If he couldn't be honest with her about who he was and what he did, then he could be honest tonight with his body.

By moonlight he led her to the bedroom where her Aunt Lila had turned down the covers and plumped the pillows before she left. But Graham didn't turn on the light by the big bed. It wouldn't help Casey, and suddenly he knew it would be wrong to illuminate the room.

Graham didn't waste time. He couldn't separate the sting of his bullet wound from the throb of his arousal, the strong beat of his heart. His whole body hurt.

In the pitch-dark he folded Casey in his embrace, tried not to notice that his wounded arm had stiffened up.

Tonight, he would make love to Casey as she'd never been loved before. Through all the lonely years of being shipped from relative to relative, even moving from place to place as an adult with Graham, she had never been cared for like this.

He couldn't admit his feelings. He didn't know if he should even try to recapture her love. When the danger was over, they might truly be over, too. But she was never going to feel again that she didn't matter.

When Graham drew her close, then followed her down onto the soft goose-down feather bed, he sighed with a contentment he hadn't felt in what seemed like forever. As if he'd been away from Casey that long. He slipped off his shoes, then hers, and dropped them onto the wooden floor. He took a moment to nuzzle Casey's throat, her breasts.

His wounds didn't hurt now, even if his lower body did.

"Babe," he whispered in her ear as he divested Casey of the rest of her clothes. "It's just us. Nothing else gets in the way, agreed?"

Her voice sounded husky, full of need, but still she hesitated. "Graham, I'm not sure we should…"

"I am." He stripped off his own shirt and pants, his briefs and Casey's one remaining garment. When her panties drifted to the floor, he wrapped her tight, and naked, in his arms.

Graham rocked against her, letting his skin warm hers, letting her feel how much he wanted her.

God, he wanted her.

"If we don't," he said with a half laugh that vibrated against her skin, "I'm in serious trouble here."

Casey smiled in the dark. "We can't have that. Not after you saved my life again today."

Graham froze. Was that all she wanted from him? Maybe so.

Their marriage hadn't been exactly a relationship between equals, not when one of them was living a lie.

Graham knew exactly how to change that.

He had always loved her in the light.

This time, he kept the room dark.

"You know how you told me that after your accident your senses became sharper?"

"Yes." She sounded puzzled by the apparent change of topic.

It wasn't, really. Graham moved over her. He nudged against the opening of her body with the tip of his shaft. Letting her feel his arousal and how much he wanted her.

"Tonight," he murmured, "the lights are out. I can't see, either. We only have each other—and hearing, taste, smell. Touch me, Case, like I'm touching you."

Despite the need crawling through him, Graham slowed his body to match the tempo Casey set. He ran his hands all over her, savoring the silk of her hair and the satiny skin of her breasts. Moving lower, he left a trail of hot kisses down her belly as he caressed the crisp curls between her thighs, kneaded her strong calves and cradled the delicate bones of her ankles. Then he worked his way back up, pausing for a long time in between to kiss her most private place, until she was gasping, pleading.

"Now, Graham. Please. I need you. Inside me."

"I need you too, babe."

And as he'd asked, she touched him in the same way—stroking her hands over him, murmuring as she held him, harder still, in her hands. The darkness made her motions more erotic. The scent of Casey's skin, the taste of her pebbled nipples, the sound of her breathing, growing more and more desperate to match the rasp of his, heightened the anticipation.

By the time Graham slid inside the smooth, slick heart of her, he felt so much pleasure he thought he might die of it.

And what if he did?

Or what if, because of Al-Hassan, this was their last night on earth?

For tonight, the danger didn't even show up on the score card. He and Casey had no differences, no barriers. On a scale of one to ten, he hit twenty-five, easy.

Too soon, he couldn't hold back any longer. When the climax ripped through him, Graham shouted his release. At the same instant Casey reached the peak with him. Graham poured himself into her, shuddering as they merged in a dark, erotic world all their own.

Chapter Twelve

"You awake, babe?" Graham nuzzled her hair.

In the afterglow of lovemaking, sometime during the night, Casey snuggled against his warm body and smiled. She burrowed deeper into the secure cradle of his arms.

"Halfway. I'm not ready to give up my dream."

She didn't say what dream, and he didn't ask. Yet Graham seemed to know. Maybe, she thought, with her pulse climbing, they shared the same one.

Maybe, when this was all over, they could even make a new start.

On the other hand, maybe they had no future. Together or apart. If the killer found them, they had few defenses. Aunt Lila's remote guest cottage, the long driveway and the trees that hid them from view, were all that kept Casey and Graham from further danger. That and his gun.

Yet if they didn't find the killer before he found them, and these *were* their last hours, Casey knew she'd leave the world happy. She'd allowed herself one more exquisite time in Graham's arms, and her body still hummed from their lovemaking.

Not just sex, she realized. Love.

There was no use denying that, even to herself. The notion had scared her once, but Casey wrapped around him now like a Christmas package with a big red-heart bow.

"Graham..." she started, in that way women had of opening a conversation about the relationship.

"Let's not," he whispered in her ear, sending a shiver of delight and renewed desire down Casey's bare spine anyway. "We can talk tomorrow. While you're helping me figure out this whole mess."

Deflated, she struggled to keep her voice casual. "Do you think the man who tailed us can tell someone where we are?"

Graham yawned. "He didn't look in any shape to talk. Besides, he wouldn't know. We ditched him—literally—ten miles from here."

"But he could—they could—make an educated guess."

He raised up on one elbow, his chest brushing her breast, sending a shiver of fresh awareness through her.

"Casey, we didn't see another car until we turned in your Aunt Lila's drive." He didn't sound as confident as Casey wanted him to be about their safety, but she made only another brief protest before Graham shifted his body to lie again over hers. As a distraction from further talk?

"I just have the feeling we're not alone."

She could sense the smile in his voice.

"We're alone, babe. And you know what?"

When he ground his hips against hers, Casey smiled again, too. "What?"

"I feel like…joining forces all over again." He had slipped into her before Casey took another breath, which came out as a groan.

For most of the night, they pleasured each other in unforgettable ways. In the hot, streaming shower of Aunt Lila's tidy bathroom. In the kitchen, against the counter, where they had trooped, smothering laughter like naughty children, to heat Lila's dinner. Then, on the sofa, on their way through the living room. And, finally, back in the big bed, where they made exquisitely slow love for hours. All the while she tried to forget about a killer, tried to tell herself that when the danger ended, they would get another chance.

"Even our honeymoon wasn't this exciting, this passionate," Casey said, though it had been close.

But then, in Barbados, a killer hadn't been after them, intent upon taking her life. And now, they believed, Graham's, too. Which intensified their reactions.

She couldn't seem to separate the hot insistence of his body in hers from the fear she still felt that she could lose him all over again.

Suddenly, the subject seemed all-important.

"Graham, please tell me more—about you."

He tensed above her but didn't answer. After a long moment, he blew out a breath. And groped again for her mouth.

"We're almost there," was all he said.

Knowing the truth would have to wait, Casey gave herself up to his passionate demand, yet she couldn't forget, even in Graham's embrace, that their lives were still in danger.

That someone wanted them dead.

By the time they fell asleep in each other's arms, Casey's brain still hummed, like her well-loved body. She stared, wide-eyed, at the ceiling where the lazy fan spun a slow breeze over her naked skin.

Like her lover's touch.

Or a killer's?

THE NEXT TIME Casey woke, she was alone.

In her world of darkness, she slipped from bed, drew on a shirt she found hanging over the brass foot rail, then padded carefully into the living room. She could hear Graham's fingers flying over Jackie Miles's computer keys.

Casey found him at the desk in the corner, off to one side of a front window, with a good view, she imagined, of the approach to the cottage. Maybe they could talk now.

From behind, she wound her arms around his

neck, but the typing continued. "I thought you were sleeping."

"Couldn't," he said. "I got to wondering what Jackie left on her computer." He paused. "I hope you don't mind."

"I don't mind. Exactly." Casey planted a kiss on his glossy dark hair. She leaned closer, to feel his muscled strength, his heat, but most of all the mingled scents of their lovemaking. It made her part of Graham. A part she didn't want to let go of so soon. Casey realized she was in a different kind of trouble now.

It was on the tip of her tongue to say "I love you"—because she did, all over again—when Graham straightened with a soft curse.

"What?" Casey said, drawing back a little.

The keys clicked again in rapid succession.

"Jackie Miles interviewed a guy who works at Hearthline. Eddie Lawton, remember? He's the computer kid we ran into there. Our tech support. To the max. I think he lives at the agency. He can fix anything. He sure fixed Jackie's setup all right." Graham tapped the screen. "They didn't just drink a few beers together after work. He hacked her right into the databases at the Pentagon."

"But why?"

"That's what I'd like to know. Eddie was lying, and this isn't part of her work for Hearthline."

Casey stood by his shoulder, tense. *The Penta-*

gon? Was Graham only trying to divert Casey now by pretending ignorance of Jackie's computer contents?

"After getting stranded at the institute, I didn't know whether to trust Jackie. But I never imagined she was trying to penetrate federal secrets." Casey's brain went on higher alert. Graham had been Jackie's partner. What did Graham have to do with the Defense Department?

He sighed. She could feel him rub the back of his neck, a habit when he was distracted. Or frustrated. Casey took over the job, kneading the tight muscles between his shoulders, hoping he'd talk.

"So," he finally said, his head dropped low for her massage. "Jackie wasn't what I thought. Or hoped she was." He groaned at Casey's soothing motions. "Keep going. That feels great. I always thought Jackie was just sloppy sometimes in her work. I guess I was wrong."

"A cover-up?"

He hesitated. "Maybe."

"Graham, if Jackie Miles was some kind of mole—"

"Let's not get hasty."

He tipped his chair forward, and Casey imagined him staring at the screen. The next thing he brought up made him stiffen. And convince Casey she was on the right track.

"Miles has a computer map of Washington here. With pinpoints all over D.C."

"What does that mean?"

Unfortunately, the question turned him back into a clam. Casey had overstepped her bounds. For reasons of his own, he wasn't about to tell her the truth, only enough to whet her interest. To make her suspicious of him all over again.

"I'm not sure. It's damn interesting, though." He shut down the document. So Casey wouldn't "see?" Before she learned too much? He turned in his chair to draw her close, between his spread legs. "Let's leave this for now. It's halfway to morning. You hungry again?"

Casey smiled, not quite distracted but tempted.

"I could be, but—"

"Me, too." He didn't mean the rest of Aunt Lila's apple pie. She could sense Graham's growing arousal, but for once Casey didn't respond. Her mind was still working on their puzzle.

"Graham, what if Jackie was involved with the man I saw in the elevator? What if he's part of her getting into the Pentagon's data? Then for some reason she turned against him—decided to tell you— and he killed her?"

He could be after Casey for a similar reason. She had seen someone she shouldn't have seen. Someone she ought to remember. And fear.

Casey added to her theory. "He murdered Marilee Baxter, too, so she wouldn't talk."

Graham refused to answer. To Casey's frustration, he pulled her down onto his lap and angled his lips over hers.

Talk about a cover-up.

Casey moaned, deepening the kiss. Their love-making was like a drug she'd been denied for too long, and in spite of her suspicions, she wouldn't give it up yet.

She'd also been denied Graham's love.

How did he feel about her now, beyond keeping Casey alive? Beyond their renewed, sensual experience together?

It wasn't enough, Casey thought, remembering Jackie Miles's computer.

Not when Graham himself was still lying to her.

GRAHAM LEANED BACK in his chair and took another look out the front window of the guest cottage. It was still dark, he was alone, and even the lamp in Lila's bedroom window across the yard had finally gone out.

Casey was sleeping. Before that, she'd asked hard questions, explored some close-to-the-bone theories. How much longer could he hold off telling her the truth?

Trying to preserve his fragile truce with Casey, at the same time he tried to nurture their renewed awareness of each other. Tried to maintain her innocence while he tracked the killer.

Graham didn't believe for an instant that their tail

on the road to Virginia was the kingpin in the conspiracy. He was a foot soldier, that was all. Taking
that one right opportunity to kill Casey and Graham
had been foiled.

But had he really meant to kill them?

And what about Jackie Miles?

She was dead. It also seemed she was a traitor.

Graham hadn't reacted to Casey's theory, but
his sense of betrayal ran deep. Why hadn't he
guessed that Jackie was playing him like a fish on
a line?

At the risk of Casey's life.

And the nation's security.

Labor Day was fast approaching. Al-Hassan
would make its move soon.

Graham turned back to the computer and felt his
heart rate soar. He realized he was staring not just at
a map of the city. The highlighted locations referred
to points of interest, all right, but they weren't sight-
seeing spots.

The Pentagon wasn't among them.

Graham's eyes homed in on the rest. Hearthline
itself didn't surprise him. But the FBI building did,
as well as CIA headquarters at Langley. He recognized its station office in D.C.

His pulse sped faster. The Hearthline leak was
only the start. Was he looking at an overall, even bigger plan to destroy government function at the intelligence level this time? If Al-Hassan hit the targets

Jackie had marked on the map, communications would be fractured, destroyed. Chaos would ensue.

His mouth went dry. He doubted Eddie Lawton was part of the conspiracy. More likely, Jackie had used him.

Her failure to meet Casey had been no oversight. If he was right, Jackie must have tipped off Casey's attacker. Whoever Jackie worked for then must have followed Casey to the subway. Isolated her even more. Threatened her. Willy had probably been a deterrent to real harm, but the message had come across.

Next time you're dead.

Had they only been toying with her? But until when?

Who in hell else was Graham looking for?

When Casey appeared in the doorway to the living room, rubbing sleep from her eyes, he felt his heart turn. And his conscience.

"Hey, babe."

"You're working too hard," Casey murmured.

Her tantalizing body turned him hard in another heartbeat. Her beautiful green gaze, so empty of the truth she sought, nearly made him lose his mind. The fresh memory of the night they'd shared, of his body buried to the hilt in hers, sent guilt crashing through him. It was his fault she'd gotten caught up in this.

Whoever she had seen before the hit-and-run must know that she might connect him to Graham.

And Hearthline.

His blood chilled.

From the moment Casey had spied that guy in the elevator, the man must have guessed Graham was most likely in the building, too. Her life had been in danger. And Graham's cover had been blown, just as he'd feared.

Why not kill them, then?

It wasn't a matter, he realized, of the right opportunity. Did he know Casey couldn't recognize him? Had Jackie passed along that information, too?

Casey didn't step closer, probably because he'd pushed her away from his investigation before.

A search that was going nowhere fast.

"I've hit a brick wall." He could use the help she'd offered. "You know the box Anton 'lost' in his apartment?"

"Yes."

"Its contents are in my duffel. Can you bring me something?"

"I think so." She sounded pleased. He had given her something to do, but he was also letting her in, a little.

"I hope there's an old picture of some people," he said. "Maybe one of them will be what I need."

Because whether he wanted her to be involved or not, Casey was the one person he knew he could trust right now.

He hated dragging her deeper into this, but he

needed all the help he could get. Afterward, he'd explain. Everything.

If they were still alive.

CASEY PLOWED THROUGH Graham's belongings.

The very stuff that had started all her troubles.

The fact that they seemed to be his troubles, too, hadn't escaped her. Neither did the presence of his gun.

Tired, yet still tingling from the long night in Graham's arms, she pushed the gun back inside and rubbed her eyes. Not that it would do any good.

The realization didn't shatter Casey as it had, not long ago, in her doctor's office. As it would have even when she and Willy encountered her attacker in the subway.

Maybe she was learning to live with her blindness.

And to believe again in Graham?

Casey still had her suspicions. But he would tell her in his own time. After she helped him solve the puzzle.

Digging in the duffel, she felt her fingers close around a small album. Pictures. The plastic quilted cover opened to reveal a dozen or so photographs encased in sleeves. Casey could feel the edges of the prints between the pages. This must be what Graham was looking for.

Another quick shuffle through the bag told her it was the only collection of photos inside.

Casey flipped through them.

She blinked…and felt her pulse kick up.

She hadn't seen a thing, except shadows or an occasional blur of movement, in weeks.

Yet there it was.

She stared down at the book in her hands, and saw people. *Faces.* They remained unclear, but there they were. She could *see* them. Eyes, noses, chins…

"Graham!" she cried out.

Oh, what she wouldn't give, especially after last night, to see his face again.

The image in front of her took firmer shape.

In their brief clarity, the faces startled her.

A group of men. Ragged clothes. Unkempt hair. Beards. They clustered around each other, around a teepee of guns stacked together, barrels up. The country around them appeared wild, mountainous. A foreign place. Like Tibet. No, Afghanistan.

They all wore a familiar look. Casey had seen it before, she realized, and it always surprised her on Graham's face. It was a restless look, full of danger and delight, a look that stared death in the face. And laughed.

He drove too fast. Always with that same light in his eyes, as if it were his rare chance now to experience risk.

A chill raced over her skin.

Was her ex-husband one of these men? How many more secrets did he have?

Casey brought the photograph closer, almost to her nose. The images had begun to blur and her heart sank in disappointment. For one instant she had hoped…. She blinked again, hard, trying to clear her sight.

Graham didn't seem to be among the group. Maybe he'd taken the picture. But one other face stood out.

Even becoming more blurred by the second, it drew Casey and she realized she had seen that man before.

The man in the elevator.

If Graham had kept the picture, if he'd taken it in the first place, then he knew the man, too.

Heart pounding, Casey scrambled to her feet. In her haste to tell Graham, she forgot the duffel bag still on the floor. Casey walked right into it. And fell.

Mortified, as she had been when she missed the kitchen step, she sat there for a moment, letting her pulse settle. Chiding herself. She really had to be more careful. More aware of her surroundings.

Casey came up on her knees. Whatever vision she'd glimpsed for the past few moments was gone. The blackness had descended again. *These things take time.*

Graham's belongings had spilled out onto the floor, and she tucked the album in her waistband before she scooped them up. When a hard item imprinted itself on her knee, she sat back on her heels and massaged the pain. Then she picked up the metal piece she'd knelt on.

"Casey?" Graham called from the other room.

"I'm coming."

Heart thumping, she turned it over in her palm. Felt its pebbled surface. Gold? And bits of stone. Ruby. Sapphire. Diamond. Red, white and blue. She couldn't see its colors, but she couldn't mistake its star shape.

She had held one just like it before.

The cuff link from Marilee Baxter's hand.

This one belonged to Graham. Where was the other?

Casey groped through the duffel but came up empty.

She might be wrong—she could have missed it— but she didn't think so. If this cuff link was the mate of the one found in Marilee Baxter's hand, why would Graham let her see that other lone cuff link?

Maybe he'd been testing her, to gauge whether she'd remember. But why? What if he had lost it during the murder? Then taken it from the crime scene to protect himself?

Her heart threatened to beat out of her chest.

Jackie Miles had been his partner.

But in what, exactly?

Was Graham himself part of the conspiracy to kill her?

Chapter Thirteen

In the living room, waiting for Casey to return, Graham pored over the list of operatives who had comprised the original antiterrorist, twelve-member task force.

Jackie hadn't investigated her share of the names before she was murdered.

Which one was in Washington now, a killer without a name or face?

Frustrated, he pushed the list aside and turned his attention to other possible suspects. Graham had eliminated DeLucci. He didn't get along with the man. But that didn't make him an assassin.

DeLucci hadn't had time to get from the diner where Jackie was killed, back to Hearthline before Graham arrived. DeLucci hadn't known Casey was Graham's ex-wife, and in Graham's experience DeLucci didn't lie. He was strictly a by-the-book kind of guy. Like Eddie Lawton, the computer tech, Hearthline's second-in-command had never been part of Graham's original team, and thus, DeLucci had never owned a pair of the memorial gold cuff links. If he was involved in the security leak and a terrorist conspiracy, he wasn't its ringleader, either.

He dismissed both men. DeLucci was a true paper-pusher, and Lawton was a somewhat smug, gee-whiz techno geek who liked to believe he was on the inside track at Hearthline. And with Jackie, perhaps romantically. Neither was the man Graham wanted.

David Wells was another matter.

From Graham's search of his ex-teammate's finances, he'd learned that large sums of money had turned up in Wells's accounts over the past few months. Graham felt he was on the right track. Some of that cash had come from an organization known to be an Al-Hassan supporter. He'd have to collar Wells again.

"Graham."

Casey's voice halted his mental hunt for the killer—and sent a fresh wave of need through him. Then alarm prickled the back of his neck. She didn't sound right. Their closeness in the past hours had disappeared, to be replaced by something dire.

"Yeah, babe." He lifted a hand. "Find the photos?"

Casey stayed in the doorway that led to the bedroom. Even from that distance, Graham could see some object tucked into her waistband. It appeared to be an album, but he could see what else she held in the palm of her hand.

"I found your cuff link, too."

Surprised, he stood and walked toward her.

To his even greater astonishment, Casey sank against the doorframe as if to evade him. With the motion, her breasts became more prominent, and despite her mood, he felt himself harden.

"My cuff links," he said. "You knew I had a pair. What's the problem?"

"One of them," she corrected. "Tell me I'm wrong, Graham. That the other cuff link wasn't in Marilee Baxter's hand when she died."

"What are you saying?" He would have cupped her cheek, soothed her, but Casey plastered herself deeper to the wood frame. He dropped his hand. "You think *I* killed her?"

"There was one cuff link in the bag. I checked twice."

"That doesn't make sense. And you know it. If I murdered her, why would I show you the other cuff link in the first place? I would have taken it from her hand then got rid of it. I wouldn't want you to ever see it."

"'See it?'" she said. "Or maybe letting a blind woman know about the cuff link made perfect sense. It threw me off base. And posed no threat. What could I do about it?"

She knew as well as he did that she wasn't helpless. The past hours in Casey's arms still had his body vibrating with sensation. The soft brush of her eager mouth, the feel of her breasts in his hands, the perfect fit of their bodies, together…her cries of completion that had matched his. She'd stayed with him all the way.

"I was with you," he told her, "when we found Marilee Baxter in that garage."

"*After* she was killed. You could have gone there earlier, while I was at the institute."

"More theories?" His mouth tightened. His arousal ebbed. "Casey, at the agency you found me at my desk. After that, we were together—all night. According to the autopsy, and her time of death, I must have been with you when Marilee Baxter died."

"That's a neat alibi, Graham. The assassin could have been a hired gun. Hired by you."

He gaped at her. "What is this? Your idea of pushing me away? Destroying what we had a few hours ago—" he swept out a hand "—in this very room, in that bed in there, in Lila's kitchen?" When she turned with a gasp, Graham swung her around. "You've made your accusations. Now let me finish. You ran away once before. You left me flat because you didn't like the work hours I kept or the business trips I had to take. You even imagined I was having some affair. You didn't give us a chance!"

"Because you wouldn't tell me the truth!"

"And you think that's because I didn't care?" He caught her shoulders. "That's some holdover from your wacky childhood. Are you afraid of a killer now? Of me? Or," he said, "of *us*?"

She bowed her head. "I don't know."

Graham pried the cuff link from her cold fingers.

"I lost the other one of this pair years ago. I tossed this one in a box of jewelry that I never wore anyway. I couldn't throw it out because, yes, it meant something to me. I haven't seen it since then. If you hadn't brought that stuff to me at Hearthline, if Anton hadn't finally remembered where he stashed it after the hit-and-run—"

She raised her head. "Rafe found the box."

"Whatever. I would never have thought of it again."

"Until Marilee Baxter died!"

"Yeah," he admitted, "until then. Not because I was involved. Because her murder, and the cuff link in her hand will lead to someone I know."

He took a breath.

"Someone I worked with," Graham admitted.

Hell. He had no choice now. No time left. Casey's lack of faith in him, her new fear that he could be the enemy who wanted her dead, stunned him. So many lies, he thought. Too many.

Damn the Counterterrorism Attack Team.

Damn the throbbing wound in his arm.

He hurt like hell. Did she also think he'd set up that chase yesterday? Nearly gotten himself killed to forge a cover so he could get her alone then kill her?

How could she think that?

He wanted to save his country.

He also wanted to save his life. With Casey.

Graham took another, deeper breath. When he opened his mouth, there would be no going back.

"Your suspicions are true. I'm an operative, babe." At the admission he watched shock take over her face. "I have been since we met. The task force I belonged to in Houston, and other places, wasn't part of 'this agency or that.' It wasn't about loans to rebuild damaged homes or businesses. It was to find the terrorists responsible for bombing the federal court there. Other attacks, as well. I was recruited right after college."

"You're a *spy*?"

"Well, sort of." He tried to explain. "Even I don't know who funds C.A.T. Few people do."

She looked puzzled.

"The Counterterrorism Attack Team—my current job. My real job." When she said nothing, he confessed, "I know this hasn't been fair to you. Maybe I should have bought you a drink in that Manhattan restaurant when we met then let it go. But I couldn't," he said. "I wanted you." Graham held her empty gaze, willing her to accept him. "The people I work for find that inconvenient. They don't care much for home and family. They can't afford to." He moved closer, touched her arm. "If a man makes that choice for himself, they turn a blind eye. And hope that doesn't compromise some mission. But it's his problem. It was mine."

Her tone cooled, like the feel of her skin.

"I don't need to be your 'problem,' Graham."

"I know. I messed up." He glanced around the room. Took another look out the windows. In an hour dawn would break. And someone might find them. She had to be on his side then. "I'm sorry, Case. More sorry than I can tell you."

But she wasn't ready to let him off the hook.

"What kind of operative?"

"Secret. Undercover. My work for C.A.T. at Hearthline—under the alias of Greg Wilcox—is critical right now. DeLucci isn't that forgetful. My assignment is to find a security breach that, unfortunately, involved you, too. What happened in the parking garage that day should never have occurred."

"Only I got in the way."

"Yeah. My fault there, too." He would always feel responsible for her blindness. To his surprise, Casey didn't quite agree.

"You told me not to go there. I didn't listen."

"And I shouldn't be telling you this now. But I need you with me, Casey. C.A.T. is hunting for the key to a terrorist conspiracy that could cost a great number of people their lives. That's what the map Jackie has on her computer is about. If I don't crack this thing soon—"

Her eyes widened. "Then it was *never* just about me."

He shook his head, forgetting she couldn't see

the motion. "No. Only because you saw someone. That someone, I'm sure, is a member of my own team—at least the team I started out with. And the worst thing I can imagine is betrayal by the man I once trusted with my life."

"Me, too," Casey murmured.

With a sad expression, she stepped past him. Then paused. From the waistband of her jeans, she handed him the small album that Graham recognized. "The pictures you wanted." Then she inched her way toward the kitchen.

Graham watched her go, memorizing the lithe beauty of her figure, the sheen of overhead light on her hair. He felt something break inside as Casey got farther from his touch, from *him,* with every step.

She still didn't have faith in him.

Yet he'd done all he could. He'd given himself away.

Graham crushed the cuff link in his fist then returned to Jackie's computer, to the cell phone records she had also left undone.

Somewhere, in that batch of numbers, was the connection he needed. To a man he had trusted. And to Casey.

Until this was done, he didn't have a chance to win her love.

GRAHAM WAS STILL staring at the maze of call records when his own cell chirped.

He silenced the ring before it could trill again.

Maybe someone had found Willy. The phone had been frustratingly silent until now. His posters hadn't worked.

"Graham?" Instead he heard Holt Kincade's voice.

Cautious, Graham didn't respond.

"I'm not asking where you are," Holt said. "I've been thinking about the gold cuff link."

"You tossed my house." Kincade didn't confirm that, but Graham's spirits sank another notch. Casey feared he was trying to murder her. Holt would find and arrest him for withholding evidence. And he'd still be short one killer. One traitor.

"About the team," Holt added.

Graham's interest perked up.

He stared at the computer screen and waited for Holt to elaborate. Before he could, Graham bolted upright in his chair, as alert as Holt sounded at this too-early hour. He swore under his breath.

The same number repeated down the current page. Two dozen times, or more. It was a cell phone belonging to Marilee Baxter's boyfriend. The man who had disappeared with the dark sedan registered in his fake name that may have struck Casey. The man who had most likely committed murder in a manner that every member of Graham's team would know.

That included Holt.

Now Graham had another choice to make. Stone-

wall Kincade again. Or invite his help. If he kept his
mouth shut, he could only hope to keep Casey alive
on his own. Graham didn't hesitate.

This must be his day for coming clean.

"Kincade. Listen to this."

The name Brian Dunlap had seemed vaguely familiar to Graham on the phony car registration, yet
he still couldn't place it. He repeated the name now
for Holt and waited for his reaction.

"The guy we think killed Marilee Baxter?"

"Yeah."

Holt's silence made Graham's nerves start to
shred. "I worked with a guy who used the name Dunlap as a cover," Holt finally offered. "I don't recognize Brian, though."

"I do," Graham said, his excitement growing. His
hunch had been right. He'd had to trust Holt in order
to find the other half of the ID. "My partner, before
I worked with Jackie Miles, used Brian instead of his
real name."

"Speaking of Jackie Miles…" Holt began.

"I was there," Graham admitted, his tone
somber. "The shooter drove a dark SUV." Maybe
the same one that had chased Graham and Casey
through Virginia. Maybe not. "I'll tell you everything I know. Later. Right now, we need to find
Brian Dunlap."

"So this guy combined the two names into one
alias."

Graham fumbled through the papers on the table for the album Casey had left with him. He flipped through it until he was looking at the photo taken in the foothills of mountains halfway around the world. Graham had snapped it himself before he knew Casey. Among the group of local agents they'd used, was another operative, a member of the original task force.

His own partner. Another betrayal.

"Tom Dallas," Graham murmured into the phone.

"You got it. Now to find him."

"I tracked down some of the old team but I'm still working on that. I never got to Tom." Graham frowned. "In part, because he's supposed to be in Afghanistan."

"If we're right, then he's not. He must be here."

Graham decided to go for broke. He needed backup.

"We're in Virginia." He gave Holt the directions to Lila's guest cottage. "Get some people out here, will you? Quick. I don't think we'll be alone much longer."

When Graham hung up, he dialed the local police, then decided to take yet another chance.

He needed all the talent he could get.

At the other end of the line Rafe Valera sounded wide-awake. He didn't hesitate.

"If Casey's in danger, I'm there."

"We may just see how good you are with that .357."

Rafe was still chuckling when Graham disconnected. The same excitement that coursed through his body now, he'd also heard in Valera's voice. Then his own smile died.

Graham remembered Casey's words. *I just have the feeling we're not alone.* Was she right? Had someone found them already, before help arrived? Graham stared at the cell phone in his hand. A second later, he had pried it apart and dumped the battery out into his hand. Son of a bitch, he thought. Along with the battery, he saw a GPS transmitter.

His heart beat hard. Never mind the dark-clothed driver of the SUV. He and Casey had been tracked from Washington, and for how long before that? Had Jackie Miles switched the original battery, replacing it with the GPS tracer? It would have been simple. She'd borrowed his phone a dozen times. Graham's every movement had been monitored by Al-Hassan. The enemy knew where he and Casey were right now, to the exact coordinates on a map.

He hadn't slammed the phone down on the desk before the lights suddenly went out and Graham was plunged into darkness.

In the too-silent house, he listened. But heard no sound except for the heavy beat of his own pulse. He couldn't see two feet in front of his face.

They weren't alone.

And he didn't know where Casey was.

IN THE BEDROOM Casey had tried to sleep.

She couldn't.

Her quarrel with Graham kept playing through her mind. His real job, his cover name, the bigger conspiracy that made her own life seem far less important....

Was he telling the truth?

Or just another lie?

Something brought her senses into sharp focus. Casey cocked her head in the direction of the living room. Graham's computer keys had stopped clacking. His low phone conversation with someone had ended.

She slipped from bed.

Neither of them would sleep for the rest of the night. It must be close to dawn by now. She would make coffee, hear everything from Graham. Then she would decide whether to believe him.

Casey wasn't sure what to believe. About Graham. About their relationship. During the night in his arms, she'd begun to hope. But was she only being gullible because she loved him?

Casey bumped into a chair, scraping the leg along the floor. She steadied it then moved forward again. The sharp noise had sounded loud.

Why was the house otherwise so quiet?

The utter stillness made her skin crawl.

Had Graham left the house?

Casey wanted to peer out the front windows, to

be sure his car was there, but of course she couldn't.
She wished again for Willy's comforting presence.

She'd made Graham angry.

But he'd hurt her, too.

In anger, had he left her alone now?

Casey crept toward the living room.

When a sharp bark from the yard startled her, she
reached out, grabbing the wall for support.

Willy?

It was wishful thinking. He couldn't be here. How
would he make the trip from Washington to Virginia
on his own? She remembered Graham's mention of
other animals, dogs and cats, finding their way home
over thousands of miles. But she doubted Willy
could track her to a place he'd never been.

She must have heard a neighbor's dog.

If only she could *see*....

But her brief flirtation with restored vision didn't
try to seduce her again. Like the strong feel of Graham's arms around her, her sight was gone.

If Graham had abandoned her and if someone
else was in the house now, could she save herself?

If someone tried to kill her, how would she defend
herself? How could she escape?

Casey's heart pounded hard.

The dog outside barked again, high and sharp.

Oh, please. Let it be Willy.

They'd had not a single call in response to the
posters that hung all over her Dupont Circle neigh-

borhood. Maybe all this time Willy had been on his way. She couldn't trust Graham completely because of all the lies he'd told her, but she did trust Willy.

Casey slipped through the living room to the rear door. She had her hand on the knob when a hard body hauled her back. A strong arm clamped around her throat. A callused palm covered her mouth.

Casey struggled but she couldn't scream.

Chapter Fourteen

"It's me," Graham whispered hoarsely in her ear.

Her heart thundered in her chest. Casey didn't know whether to feel relieved or even more afraid.

She heard her own breath, short and ragged.

"Willy's outside." Quickly Graham filled her in. "He didn't get here by himself." His hand was still clamped over her mouth and Casey could taste his skin, smell his scent. She whimpered against the restraint. Graham squeezed her as if in reassurance but didn't let her go. "You were right. We're not alone. The lights just went out. Probably the landline phone is cut too," he said. "That's why Willy was barking. To warn us." Graham's mouth hovered close, sending an unwanted thrill along her skin. "Are you with me, Case?"

I need you.

She heard it in his voice. Or was it the echo of her own thought?

There was no more time.

She had to make her choice now.

Based on what? Casey wondered. Sheer emotion? The fact that when he touched her, as he had all night, she wanted nothing more than to do whatever he asked? What if Graham won her trust, then drew her into the trap? If he was part of the terrorist conspiracy, then like a lamb to the slaughter she would be led to her own death.

Yet it was Casey's lack of faith that had helped to destroy their marriage.

You didn't give us a chance.

If she didn't believe him now, not only would her life be at risk, the nation's security would be, too.

Unless he was lying to her again....

Graham pressed her to the wall beside the kitchen door. She felt the hard strength of his body but something more, as well. She sensed Graham's need. She sensed truth.

It was time. Time to let go of her past, the painful childhood that had set her up for mistrust. Casey frowned. Yet Aunt Lila had welcomed her with open arms. She would have to think about that. Later. Remembering last night's lovemaking with Graham instead, Casey made her choice.

Are you with me?

Vigorously, she nodded.

Outside, Willy barked again. Calling to her.

She needed to go to him.

When Graham released her, she gazed blankly

into his eyes. Wanting so badly to see what she most needed. His love.

In the dark, he couldn't see now any better than she could. But neither could their assailant.

"Willy can help," she mouthed. Eager to see him, she reached again for the doorknob.

Again, Graham covered her hand with his. Hard.

"No! That's why I had to catch you before you opened this door. I already found a GPS transmitter hidden in my cell phone, Casey. Our every move has been tracked. Willy could be booby-trapped. You welcome him inside, which is just what our guy wants you to do—and in the next nanosecond we get blown to bits. Plastique, C-4, who knows? It doesn't take much."

Feeling helpless, Casey caught her lower lip between her teeth. What could they do? Obviously, Graham knew more than she did about explosives, firearms, stealth.

Silent, like a wraith, he slipped across the kitchen. Making barely a sound, he slid open a drawer then returned to Casey.

"Lila's butcher knife could use a good sharpening, but it'll do for now." Casey recoiled from the blade. She didn't doubt Graham knew how to use it. He steered her toward the living room again. "Think you can make it to the bedroom without giving us away? You'll have to be careful. I need my bag. I want you to get my gun."

"Graham—" she whispered, unsure she could help.

"You can do it, babe."

Still, she hesitated. What if she slammed into a chair or fell over her own clothes on the bedroom floor? As if he sensed her self-doubt, Graham cupped the back of her neck.

A flood of need, mingled with fear, washed through her body. Casey struggled to find courage. If she didn't do her part, they would die. Willy, too, perhaps.

Graham tipped the balance.

"It's dark as hell in here, Case. This time I need you to be my eyes."

FOR THE FIRST TIME, total darkness became her ally.

The enemy now wasn't her lost eyesight. Or Graham.

In the blackness she crept through the living room then into the bedroom. Keeping low. Away from the windows. She didn't imagine for a moment that Willy was outside in the yard, alone. Graham stayed close but let Casey do the maneuvering. Ironically, he was far more likely than she to trip over something. Anything.

Would they make it?

Casey wished she'd had more training at the institute. With time, she would be able to manage most of her life without assistance, except from Willy. If he survived. Was the possible timer rigged to go off before she located Graham's gun?

Casey nearly sobbed with frustration.

Near the dresser, she fumbled for Graham's duffel. When she found it, she slid open the zipper, holding her breath when it rasped along the track. The slight noise sounded like a whole fireworks display. She stopped to listen but still heard nothing.

Good.

She had her hand on the butt of Graham's gun, ready to pull it out, when she sensed movement behind them.

Before Casey could react, a hard male voice she didn't recognize said, "Freeze, Warren. You, too, baby." She heard the sound of a gun being cocked. "Make a false move and lover boy dies. Looks like your skills are rusty, Warr—or should I say Wilcox?"

He had Graham! Casey did as she was told. And froze.

A familiar scent reached her nostrils, making her heart pound. *The man in the elevator.*

"TOM DALLAS. You son of a bitch," Graham said mildly.

His ex-partner flicked on a light. Graham glanced back to see his eyes narrowed, an icy, emotionless blue. His blond hair was shorter now, but otherwise he hadn't changed much in appearance since the last time Graham had seen him. Fair hair, he thought. Unremarkable. It was Casey's description of the man she'd seen in the elevator. Why hadn't Graham realized sooner who that was?

"Hey. I brought your dog back, didn't I? What are partners for? Thought I'd give you a sporting chance, a sign that I was here, too. You must remember. I like animals."

"I remember you wanting to roast someone's pet Akita over a campfire in the Japanese Alps."

Dallas had always harbored a cruel streak. He made a *tsk*-ing sound, and Graham knew he would have no qualms about killing Willy, killing anyone who got in his way. In fact, that's why he had come.

"Good memory, but let's not scare the little lady." He shoved Graham toward her. "Take your hand out of the duffel bag, please, Mrs. Warren. A gun won't do you any good."

The worst betrayal I can imagine is by the man I once trusted with my life.

"Hurry," he murmured, "or I'll have to hurt your husband."

Graham braced himself. When Dallas pushed him farther into the bedroom, Casey did as she was told. Her face was white, her lips pressed together. Her beautiful green eyes were downcast. She drew her hand from the duffel bag at the same time Tom Dallas, behind him, karate-chopped Graham's wrist. Lila's butcher knife clattered to the floor.

"I ought to torture you," Dallas growled. "Use

every trick in the book—everything we learned at
Langley and all those other hellholes they call 'ad-
vanced courses.' I'd have you singing like a mock-
ingbird in ten minutes. But why not take my time?"

Graham massaged his numb wrist. "Works for
me. That'll give the police and Holt Kincade's men
time to get here."

"Holt? Well, isn't this old home week? Nice try,
but I'm betting you and the missus, or should I say
ex-missus, are alone. Sorry about your divorce, by
the way."

He didn't sound sorry. Graham wondered whether
the man he'd once called his friend had any feelings.
Graham himself had suppressed his own emotions
for too long, especially where Casey was concerned.
Now because of him, her life was in grave danger.

Graham didn't see the blow coming. When the
butt of a gun struck him, he grunted in pain. Dallas
only laughed.

"That's for running my man off the road. He'll recover, no thanks to you. When I had to pick up the
trail myself, I wasn't a happy man."

Graham tried to catch his breath. "How much
trouble was that? You had a tracking device on my
cell phone."

"Ah, you found it. Good work. Don't you love sat-
ellites? They've made our business a precision art."
His voice became a snarl. "This was all unnecessary,
you know. You can blame your wife for that. If I

hadn't seen her at Hearthline, I wouldn't have guessed you were working there, at least not for a while longer."

"You struck Casey down in the parking garage."

"Regrettable. An impulse, perhaps, but I couldn't take the chance on her knowing who I was. It would be difficult to explain my presence at Hearthline that day."

"You were there to meet a contact." It wasn't a question.

He didn't answer that. "When Casey didn't die in the accident, and she didn't seem to recognize me, I decided to have some fun. Put pressure on you, Warren. Set her heart racing, frighten her into keeping her mouth shut. At any rate, whether she did or not, it gave me time."

"For treason?" Graham said tightly. "You've been the one selling secrets from Hearthline to Al-Hassan."

"With the support of David Wells, for one. We both agree, the other side holds more appeal these days. And all the while, you were inadvertently helping me."

"You've been toying with us." Turning, Graham made a frustrated sound. "How the hell could I help—"

"Jackie Miles. Or whatever her cover name was." He paused, as if uncertain he should tell them more. "At first she didn't want to cooperate, of course. But she did like the money I paid her to slow your investigation down—and funnel information to me." Dallas smiled. "Part security," he added, "part personal. Jackie let me know just what information you had, and would have told me if your wife finally remembered who I was. Lucky for her, she didn't.

"Then, too, there was my threat—to kill not only you and Casey but Jackie's family if she didn't do things my way. Strange," he murmured. "You and I have run agents like Jackie all over the world."

"Not in the U.S.," Graham said tautly.

His head ached from Dallas's blow, but he had to keep his wits about him. If he didn't, he and Casey were lost.

Dallas shrugged. "After poor Marilee died in the garage, Miles knew I meant what I said. But, sad for her, she had second thoughts. She felt guilty gathering data from, shall we say, 'classified' sources other than Hearthline." He shook his head. "Worse, she actually liked you, liked Casey. When Jackie's new scruples got in my way, I had no choice. She would have spilled her guts to you in that diner."

Graham had his own urge to kill. Jackie had been wrong, but she was only a dupe. Casey was still alive, yet Graham didn't have much time. She was crouched near his duffel bag, and he prayed she stayed there. He had to come up with a plan to save them. Keep Dallas talking.

"How could you betray the country like that? Kill

Miles and try to kill Casey who couldn't identify you?"

In response, Dallas landed a punch that knocked Graham back. He lost his balance, then fell to his knees, still weak from his bullet wound and Dallas's blows.

"Easy," the man said. "After all, that's what I'm trained to do. Now I'm going to kill you both. I've always hated you, Warren," he said in a matter-of-fact tone. "You're too honest, loyal, a real Boy Scout undercover. But my game of cat and mouse is over now. Like Marilee and Jackie, you've served your purpose." He hesitated. "It wouldn't do for me to be discovered before the Labor Day attacks. I must thank you, though. During a difficult mission, it's always good to have some comic relief."

"You bastard!" Graham cried out in fury. He struggled to his feet. "I knew one of the team was involved with Al-Hassan. I would have found you sooner, Dallas, if—"

"I wasn't more cunning than you."

"We were partners!" As he rose to his feet, Dallas kicked him in the stomach, and Graham's vision blurred. He staggered upright, spying Lila's butcher knife not far away. Could he reach it in time?

The thought hadn't left his mind before the knife spun across the wood, farther away, like a child's top. He felt his hatred for the traitor coalesce into an almost physical presence. How could he overcome the worst enemy he had ever faced?

When Dallas struck him with the gun butt again, the room swam in front of Graham's eyes. So did regret.

He tried to focus on Casey, her bent head and dark blond hair hiding her green eyes, but that's all he could do. A wave of need, and love, went through his aching body.

Like Tom Dallas, he had lived a lie.

Now he would not be able to save Casey. Again, because of him, she would suffer. He was unarmed, unable to defend her. Or himself. Without a miracle, he would fail Casey again.

And now they would die.

But Casey wasn't unarmed.

She couldn't see to guide a knife, and she couldn't see to shoot Graham's gun. She didn't have to see to help him, though. She had to help, or they would die.

In the dark she reached back into the duffel bag, praying Tom Dallas wouldn't notice. He was raging at Graham, reminding him how many ways there were to kill a man. Promising to use the slowest, cruelest one on Graham. After he killed Casey. And made Graham watch.

Tom Dallas wasn't watching now, Casey hoped. She came up on her knees, pulled her hand from the bag with something clutched tight in her fist—then let it fly and winged the single gold cuff link at his head.

His voice had given her a target.

Her aim was still wild. It didn't matter.

The diversion gave Graham time to react. Not expecting Casey to try anything, Dallas made a startled sound when the cuff link hit him. "My eye!"

Which seemed fitting, to Casey. Graham didn't waste the opportunity. She heard a short scuffle, then a satisfying whoosh of air when the breath rushed from a pair of lungs. Graham? Tom Dallas?

A split second later, to her vast relief, Graham had him on the floor. Graham was breathing hard.

"Hand me the gun, babe. I can't keep my knee on the back of his neck forever." He paused. "Although it's tempting. A slight twist—and too bad, Dallas. It's broken. You're dead."

Casey heard Graham haul him to his feet. She passed the cold-steel Glock to his waiting hand. She could imagine Graham holding it to Tom Dallas's head. "If they don't try you for treason, I'm coming after you myself."

Casey heard sharp pounding at the door. A man called out. "Warren, you there?"

"Holt Kincade," Graham said for her benefit.

"Casey?" It was Rafe Valera's voice.

"Come on in! We got him."

We. Casey thought it was the most beautiful word in the English language. After Tom Dallas went to jail, she would tell Graham, then convince him to take her back.

In the yard Willy barked his head off.

As someone took charge of Tom Dallas, she touched Graham's arm, and he covered her hand with his. "Holt brought a bomb squad unit. He'll be okay."

He meant Willy.

Casey felt the tension ebb from her body, leaving her weak with relief. The rest of her questions could wait. Her declaration of love, too. Soon enough Casey would ask them, then offer Graham her heart. For now, they were alive.

"It's over," he said.

The end of a long, dark nightmare, Casey thought. Graham gathered her into the tight, secure circle of his arms, and she decided she was never going to leave.

Not if she could help it.

For them, she hoped, this would be a new, bright beginning.

Chapter Fifteen

Graham sat with Casey, Holt Kincade and Rafe Valera around Lila's dining room table. The other two men were conducting a postmortem of that morning's events and the terrorist conspiracy in general, with Casey's eager attention.

It was true, the Labor Day attacks had been averted. Tom Dallas and his cohorts from Al-Hassan, including David Wells, were in custody. Casey was in no danger. But Graham was still frowning.

"I know the other two men I saw in the elevator with Dallas were part of the conspiracy," Casey said. "But who were they?"

"Renegades. Trained in Afghanistan where Tom first came into contact with Al-Hassan," Holt answered.

"It was Tom who ran me down. He threatened me in the Metro. But when one of those other men pushed me into the revolving door, then got away, he was driving Tom Dallas's car—with the phony registration."

"Yep," Holt agreed. "The same car that struck you. He was doin' Dallas's dirty work for him. The guy then returned to Marilee Baxter's house—"

"Which she shared with Tom Dallas," Graham supplied, trying to enter the conversation. "When his cohort got there, he and Dallas argued about the incident. Marilee overheard them."

Holt jumped in. "She threatened to call the police. She knew more than that, about your first accident, Casey, about the whole conspiracy. So Dallas decided to shut her up. Permanently."

Casey's gaze sharpened. "Then during the struggle she grabbed his cuff link. The one Graham found in her grip."

Holt snorted, his blue-green eyes twinkling. "And your would-be felon of an ex-husband kept it to himself." He looked at Graham. "You know I should run your devious ass right into a cell for withholding evidence."

"Try it."

Graham forced a smile. But Holt had a point, and Graham couldn't seem to shake his own dark mood. Everyone was having a good time, except him. Even the fact that he hadn't seen Casey smile like this, without a care, in a long time didn't help. Lila's promised rich coffee and thick slices of her chocolate cake, which they were waiting for, didn't ease his mind. Or his guilt.

"And then there's Willy," Casey went on. "It was

Tom Dallas who took him from my apartment building?"

Graham had to disagree. "No, it was Tom's man again. Remember, unlike the day in the elevator and in the Metro, you didn't smell his scent then. It turns out, you were right. It was a specially blended after-shave. Made in Kabul."

Next to him, Holt grimaced as he filled in the missing pieces for her. "And that bomb wired to Willy was no piece of cake. My team had a helluva time defusing the damn thing out in that yard." He pointed at the window.

"And not long to do it." Casey leaned down to pat Willy, who was lying on the floor at her feet, tongue lolling with that stupid grin on his canine face. It was as if he'd never been away. Or in danger himself.

Graham wished he felt like smiling but he didn't. "I thought the bomb was rigged to go off when any-one touched him," he said. "Instead it was on a timer."

"With exactly three minutes until detonation when we arrived. Willy was lucky," Holt added, smoothing his blond hair. "So were we. I'd hate to lose a man." He glanced at Casey. "Or woman. Sure you don't want to sign on, Casey? You'd make one terrific asset for counterterrorism."

Graham did smile then. "You should have seen her fire that cuff link at Dallas's head."

"I hit him in the eye," she said proudly.

"But our sharpshooter has other plans," Graham added.

He prayed they did. He had a lot to make up for.

His own blunder, for one. He'd left Washington and a high-tech home security system, only to put Casey at risk in Lila's cottage. He'd checked the door locks last night, but they were standard issue. Tom Dallas had probably slipped one without effort using a common credit card. He'd been inside with them before Graham knew what happened.

And he'd thought he could keep Casey safe.

As if the very remoteness of the cottage would be sufficient. Or the gun he carried.

As soon as they reached Lila's, he'd gone back to the car, checked it from stem to stern looking for a tracking device. Which had been right there all along on his own cell phone. Secret Agent Man. He really should retire.

"I have plans?" Casey said, her dark blond head turned in his direction.

"Yes. And they're on a need to know basis."

She started to bristle. "You're not keeping anything from me again, Graham Warren."

"—and Kincade doesn't need to know," he added.

Rafe Valera was sitting closer to her than Holt, who sat across from her. Rafe laid a brawny hand on her shoulder. "You need me to teach Graham some manners?"

She smiled, knowing he was teasing.

"I'll handle it. Him," she said.

Graham straightened in his chair. He eyed Valera's muscle-bound frame, his dark hair and eyes. Even joking, the man looked fierce.

"What is it you do, anyway?" Graham asked, irritated.

Valera shrugged. "A little of this, a little of that." He paused, as if uncertain whether to share information. Graham knew that feeling only too well. Looking around the table at each of them, Rafe finally admitted, "I've been an air marshal for the past two years."

Casey blinked. "That's why you're gone sometimes?"

"I was. I've quit, though. I needed to be available." His darker gaze focused on the wall, on a picture of Lila's. "Pop's getting worse. I've decided to find him an assisted-living place. That's why I was cleaning out the closet when I discovered that box you'd lost."

Casey laid a comforting hand on his arm.

"Oh, Rafe. I'm sorry about Anton."

At that point Lila brought their food to the table. The other two men fell on their enormous slices of chocolate cake as if they were starving. After the crisis at the cottage, they were obviously ravenous, but Graham didn't have an appetite.

When Lila took a chair, the older woman reached for Casey's hand. Lila was smiling, too, yet Graham thought her eyes looked misty.

"I looked out my window, saw those men piling into the yard, uniforms scrambling everywhere. And I couldn't believe my eyes. What was that all about?"

"It's classified," Casey murmured.

"I can tell you, ma'am, that the danger is past," Holt assured her. "My group wrapped things up— with a bit of help from the local police—and hauled away the bad guy."

"But who is he?" Lila asked.

"The man who stole my dog," Casey answered.

That surprised Graham, but Lila knew better than to pursue the matter. Half the operatives Graham knew lived in Virginia. Such vague answers were standard. *I work for the government.* Lila patted Casey's hand again.

"Whoever he was, I'm glad he didn't hurt you. And that I have this chance to apologize. When you were a little girl and spent that year with us, I wanted to keep you. I wanted to adopt you, dear." Lila hesitated. "But your uncle was already ill by then. Because of that, he thought a child would be too much for me to handle, so I had to let you go. I'm sorry," she said. "I don't want to lose you again, Casey. Or Graham," she added with a fond look. "I hope to see you both more often from now on."

Graham sipped his coffee. "I think we can arrange that," he murmured, even though he wasn't sure he'd be part of the picture. Or Casey's future.

"We can?" She glanced at him.

He had a lot of talking to do first. "I'll tell you all about it. In the meantime, your cake is at six o'clock, your napkin at nine. Don't spill the coffee. It's damn good. Look for it at two."

Lila blinked. "You spill anything you want. We'll just mop it up." Rafe grinned, but both Graham and Kincade looked away, intently focused on their dessert, because Lila's voice was tight. "Welcome home, dear. I've missed you so. Welcome home."

HAD LILA been waiting for her all along? With this warm sense of being home? Maybe, for years, it was Casey who hadn't felt wanted, when all the time she really was.

From now on, she would trust the feeling—Graham, too. With her heart, with her very being. He was, and always had been, the only man she wanted. The love of her life.

Why had he seemed so grim and troubled earlier?

Now the cottage was quiet again.

After Rafe and Holt left, Lila had insisted that Graham and Casey stay the night. They would return to D.C. tomorrow. Now, with the moonlight blanketing them in silver, she imagined, they lay side by side on the big feather bed for a second night. Casey didn't know how to approach him, but in the end, she didn't have to.

"Get over here," Graham whispered, then pulled her close. Casey buried her cheek against his chest.

Soft, firm, the perfect pillow for her.

"What's wrong?" she asked. "Tom Dallas didn't win."

"Nope."

"We foiled the terrorist attack, Graham," she

pointed out, ready to hear him say that was top secret.

"Yep."

"That's it? Just yes?" Casey kissed his throat. Now that she knew about C.A.T., Graham's secrets didn't threaten her security. "At least it's an answer."

She stared up at him in the always-dark. When she blinked, his face didn't appear as the clear image she had hoped for. Not this time. Casey's brief vision of the group photo, and Tom Dallas—the man in the elevator—hadn't been a sign after all, of restored sight.

Or was it? Perhaps....

She would see her doctor when they got home. For the moment, Casey cradled Graham's face in her hands, and remembered. His dark hair and eyes, his wonderful smile. She wanted to hear it in his voice.

If the swelling around her optic nerves finally receded, as the view of the group photo could indicate, some vision might eventually return—at least to the point where Casey would be able to see with glasses.

But if an occasional, fleeting image was all she'd ever glimpse, so be it. She had Willy, plus her own resources. As long as she could touch Graham's face, hear his voice, smell his scent, taste him on her lips, and feel his love, she would be happy.

Assuming he wanted her.

Raising himself on an elbow, Graham watched the vulnerable expression cross her beautiful face. *Well, at least that's an answer.* He couldn't tell her everything, but enough to satisfy her curiosity and keep the lines of communication between them open this time. Graham took a deep breath.

"Tom Dallas won't betray this country again. He and his men will be behind bars for the rest of their lives—if they don't get the death penalty for murder."

He smoothed back her hair, his hand trembling.

"Then what?" she said. "I know something's wrong."

"Everything," he admitted, feeling miserable. "I got you mixed up with Tom Dallas. I risked your life."

To his surprise, Casey bristled. "I was *mixed up* with Dallas when I walked into the Hearthline lobby and saw him in the elevator." She gazed up at him, blankly, not because of her sight. She didn't understand. "Tell me. How is that your fault?"

"Lila's cottage," he managed, gesturing at the room, the bed, because his throat had shut down.

Casey exhaled a breath. "It was my idea to come here."

"And you were great today, Case," he agreed.

"Well, then. We worked it out. Together."

"Yeah." His spirit lightened. "I guess we did. And I couldn't have done it without you," he acknowledged. "I guess that's a good lesson for me." Graham hesitated, staring down into her gorgeous green eyes. His voice turned husky. "Can we work out the rest, Casey? Between us?"

She blinked in surprise.

Graham swallowed. It was time to lay himself on the line. His heart. He'd been waiting all day.

"The truth of it is, I can't do much of anything worth a damn without you. In my view our divorce was a mistake." He gulped back his last fear. "So what do you say?"

"About what?" She seemed to be holding her breath.

Now that he'd begun, she wouldn't make it easy for him, and he couldn't blame her. He should be on his knees. With a new diamond ring. Begging.

"I think we should get married. Remarried."

Casey's mouth fell open.

"That is," he added, "unless you'd rather hang out with Rafe Valera."

Her eyes flashed. "There is nothing between me and Rafe except friendship. I'm glad he turned out not to be involved in the terrorism thing, but he's not my type."

Graham took the lashing. He deserved it. Maybe Tom Dallas and his terrorist conspiracy would prove to have one good effect. He hoped.

"Who is your type?"

She didn't hesitate. "You." Casey wound her arms around his neck and pulled his head low. "You exasperating man. I love you, Graham. I never stopped loving you."

"Me, too." Yet even that wasn't enough.

"I need to hear you say it, Mr. Strong and Silent."

Graham returned her watery smile. Risk, he reminded himself, was his middle name. It was what made his senses hum. Made him feel alive. That, and Casey's love.

"I thought I was the mild-mannered civil servant."

She snickered. "Yeah, right. And all along I was dealing instead with a superhero."

He sobered. *"I love you.* You don't mind what I do?"

Casey paused. "I won't mind—if we can agree that you'll share whatever you can about your work. In return, I'll try not to ask too many questions."

They grinned at each other.

"It's a deal," he said.

"My hero."

Graham groaned in relief. He would *never* lie to her again. His heart beating hard, hope pounding through him, he dropped his mouth onto hers and kissed her for a long, sweet time. Across the room Willy's tail whapped, as if in waltz time, against the floor. Casey had made him a bed of blankets near the window, but Graham's mind wasn't on the dog.

"Casey, I've made a decision."

Having nearly lost her to Tom Dallas and his crazed vision of the world, Graham knew he'd had enough of firsthand cloak-and-dagger. He was thirty four years old. Time to make a change.

She was waiting patiently.

"I've been offered a supervisory position with C.A.T. And a pay raise. I'm going to take it."

To his surprise, she frowned. "Are you sure?"

Yes. "I need time with you. For us."

"But what if you're not happy sitting behind a desk?"

"I will be. I won't jeopardize our family." He plunged on before he lost his nerve. "I want to have kids."

Obviously delighted, Casey kissed him again, wriggling her hand between them to Graham's briefs. "Then let's get started."

He caught his breath, but then shook his head.

"Uh-uh. Wedding first."

"Graham."

He grinned. "Well, maybe a rehearsal wouldn't hurt."

For long moments they busied themselves, perfecting things like technique and body language until Casey let out a heartfelt sigh. In the next second she had pulled off her nightshirt and dropped it to the floor.

Graham gazed down at her in the darkness, and felt his heart constrict. She was so beautiful and she was his. Again. When Willy joined them on the bed as if he'd been invited, Graham grunted.

"This isn't going to be a habit with him, is it?"

"I imagine so. He hates sleeping alone."

Graham swore, but without irritation. The golden retriever didn't deserve a reprimand. He'd been through enough, and he was Casey's loyal companion. Just like Graham. "I suppose he wants to be in the wedding party, too."

Casey pulled his head back down to hers. Graham felt her grin against his mouth. "Willy is our eyewitness."

He groaned—in part because Casey had just touched him where it counted most.

"That's a lousy joke."

"It's no joke, Graham. Now stop talking. Make love to your ex-wife and soon-to-be bride."

He kissed her lips. "We always were compatible."

"Especially here."

After that, silence ruled. Except for Willy's panting breaths from the nearby living room where he had retreated to give them privacy, and from the darkened bedroom, Casey and Graham's not-so-soft moans and sighs.

"A little lower," Casey whispered.

"Five o'clock?"

"Six," she said. "Ah, there."

A long time later Casey lay in Graham's arms. And counted her blessings. She was loved. And loved in return.

She didn't need her sight to be happy.

She had Graham.

Like a phantom in the night
comes an exciting promotion from

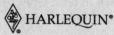

HARLEQUIN®

GOTHIC ROMANCE

Look for a provocative
gothic-themed thriller each month
by your favorite Intrigue authors!
Once you surrender to the classic
blend of chilling suspense and
electrifying romance in these
gripping page-turners, there will
be no turning back....

Available wherever Harlequin books are sold.

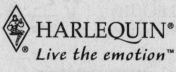

HARLEQUIN®
Live the emotion™

www.eHarlequin.com

HIE3

SPOTLIGHT

Every month we'll spotlight original stories from Harlequin and Silhouette Books' Shining Stars!

Fantastic authors, including:

- Debra Webb
- Julie Elizabeth Leto
- Merline Lovelace
- Rhonda Nelson

Plus, value-added Bonus Features are coming soon to a book near you!

- Author Interviews
- Bonus Reads
- The Writing Life
- Character Profiles

SIGNATURE SELECT SPOTLIGHT
On sale January 2005

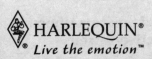

HARLEQUIN®
Live the emotion™

Silhouette®
Where love comes alive™

SPOTLIGHT

"Debra Webb's fast-paced thriller will make you shiver in passion and fear...."—*Romantic Times*

Dying To Play

Debra Webb

When FBI agent Trace Callahan arrives in Atlanta to investigate a baffling series of multiple homicides, deputy chief of detectives Elaine Jentzen isn't prepared for the immediate attraction between them. And as they hunt to find the killer known as the Gamekeeper, it seems that Trace is singled out as his next victim...unless Elaine can stop the Gamekeeper before it's too late.

Available January 2005.

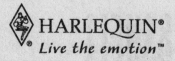

Live the emotion™

Exclusive Bonus Features:
Author Interview
Sneak Preview...
and more!